# COUNTER OPS

# COUNTER OPS

## FEDERAL AGENTS OF MAGIC™ BOOK THREE

TR CAMERON    MARTHA CARR    MICHAEL ANDERLE

This book is a work of fiction.

All of the characters, organizations, and events portrayed in this novel are either products of the author's imagination or are used fictitiously. Sometimes both.


Cover Art by Jake @ J Caleb Design
http://jcalebdesign.com / jcalebdesign@gmail.com

A Michael Anderle Production



LMBPN Publishing
PMB 196, 2540 South Maryland Pkwy
Las Vegas, NV 89109

First US edition, May 2019
Print ISBN: 978-1-64202-281-0
Version 1.03, December 2019

**Thanks to the JIT Readers**

Diane L. Smith
John Ashmore
Nicole Emens
Daniel Weigert
Dave Hicks
Kelly O'Donnell
Larry Omans
Micky Cocker

*If we've missed anyone, please let us know!*

**Editor**
The Skyhunter Editing Team

# DEDICATIONS

***From Martha***

To everyone who still believes in magic
and all the possibilities that holds.
To all the readers who make this
entire ride so much fun.
And to my son, Louie and so many wonderful friends who
remind me all the time of what
really matters and how wonderful
life can be in any given moment.

***From Michael***

To Family, Friends and
Those Who Love
To Read.
May We All Enjoy Grace
To Live The Life We Are
Called.

# CHAPTER ONE

The faint buzz of Kayleigh's drone was faintly audible over the sounds of revelry emanating from the ramshackle construction ahead. The faded metal sides and broken windows of the warehouse suggested that the structure had been abandoned. The skeleton of the building provided the perfect camouflage to hide the lawbreakers within.

*Not just any lawbreakers. Lucrative lawbreakers.*

The feed from the drone played in a small window on Diana's AR display glasses. The structure and thirty or so feet on either side were easily visible. Tony crept silently toward the back using all his years of experience as a former detective, while Cara approached from the left using the stealth tactics she'd learned in her military service. The team leader couldn't see Rath or Max. Both were well hidden somewhere on the right of the building as backup. The human members of the team had agreed that the less frequently the troll was seen with their bounty hunter personas, the better. Rath had not agreed and had insisted that he should be a part of all the missions. For training purposes, of course.

*Must train.*

He wasn't wrong. They all needed to keep their skills sharp to deal with the escalating challenges they faced. And in this case, that need resulted in a hidden troll and Borzoi ready to step in if required. The pair had talent. Diana couldn't see them on the feed at all. Her attention was pulled away from the search as the others finally reached their positions and tapped their own AR glasses to send the signal to her device that they were ready. The cursors over their positions on the overview pulsed and rippled in response.

Kayleigh's vibrant voice carried over the comms. Another benefit of scoring such a great tech was all the added support she could bring to their cover operations. Bounty hunting wasn't an easy business, after all. Once Diana had replaced the blonde's tech after their last adventure, she was only too happy to assist where she could.

"Okay, the drone shows a ton of heat signatures inside. I managed a quick dip to look in a window, and they're all behaving stupidly in there. Drinking, dancing, throwing things, and generally partying it up."

Diana made sure the sleeves of her Two Worlds Security shirt were pulled down to hide the skin where the glyphs appeared each time she used magic. Next, she tucked the cuffs under the new clunky bracelets she wore. The jewelry brought a grin to her lips. The team had watched another *Avengers* movie together when she'd noticed Black Widow's wrist weapons. That had given her the idea to pass her magic off as advanced technology.

She and Kayleigh had collaborated to fashion the ornaments. They glowed slightly when she called on her power, and it would be easy for the uninformed to assume that the results came from the mundane, rather than the magical. The other agents had simply laughed.

*They're jealous. Okay, maybe they are a little silly and possibly not that helpful, but I'll take any edge I can get. Plus, they look cool.*

Cara's voice conveyed a lack of appreciation for their quarries' antics. "Are they still partying from last night, or did they sleep and start again? It's not like the heist they pulled was particularly impressive."

Tony radiated pure sarcasm. "Come on, now. These people are criminal rock stars. Hitting three liquor stores one after the other and setting them ablaze to cover the theft? Genius."

Diana could almost hear his eyes rolling.

"If only they'd realized those places have cameras, they might have gotten away with it," he added with little remorse.

Rath chimed in. "Alcohol truck. Flames. Big bada boom."

Diana laughed. "Yes, the part where they lit their getaway vehicle on fire couldn't have been a high point of their evening. But it tells us two important things. First, they have a fire user, who we saw on the video. And second, they have someone who does water, cold, air, or something that could put it out."

Cara added, "Or one who does both."

The team leader nodded. Magic users frequently stuck

to their strengths, but more and more often, they encountered adepts skilled in multiple varieties.

*Like Nylotte would say, let it flow. It's already inside you.*

She sighed at the thought of her teacher. The training sessions with the Drow were frequent and exhausting. She felt worn out by them, so she'd jumped at the chance to do something more practical. Rounding up the group of low-level bounties that made up this particular ragtag gang would give her a nice adrenaline rush and paycheck.

*Plus, if Bryant's intel is right and they're involved in blocking our supplies, it would be worth doing at twice the hassle.*

"Is there anything else before we go, Kayleigh?" she asked.

"Nope. It's like we thought. The idiots are moving around in there, so I can't give you a plot, but the sentries are still in position." The defenders' locations pulsed softly on her AR display.

"All right, then. Rath, keep your eyes open. Tony and Cara, let's time it so we all reach the building at once and disable the guard nearest our entry point." She crept forward with purposeful deliberation, crossed quickly from cover to cover, then paused to reassess. The unexpected heat of the April day made her sweat under the heavy black shirt and the combat vest it concealed. She wore jeans, and an army-style utility belt held her automatic pistol in a right hip holster, while a taser hung from a matching one on the left. Her trusty Ruger was tucked into her custom boot and filled with anti-magic rounds. She had a spare magazine of the expensive bullets for the Sig-Sauer, but none for the rifle. All signs indicated that this wouldn't be a threat level that required it, and they had to conserve the ammunition for more important ops. The group consisted of a few magicals and a handful of morons.

*At least they had the sense to post guards.*

If they could be called that. The sentry nearest her failed miserably. The sap spent more time looking wistfully at the revelry than scanning his surroundings.

*I hope the others are equally as stupid.*

She crept behind him, grabbed his arms, and yanked him through the doorway. The taser buzzed with electricity as the guard convulsed painfully before he finally slumped against her. She released her grip on the trigger and lunged to guide the body to the ground before she delivered a sharp blow to his head that knocked him out. Her quick, "Target down," was echoed by Cara and Tony shortly thereafter.

She felt a flush of pride at the team's efficiency.

*BAM Pittsburgh kicks serious ass, and don't you forget it. Whoever you are.*

Her mental voice laughed but sounded far more mocking than amused.

*Why am I talking to myself?*

She shook her head and peeked around the small metal doorframe. The warehouse had a basic design. A large slab of concrete was bounded by a rectangle of vertical metal and covered by a slanted roof a couple of stories above. Large beams created a grid at the top that attached to regularly spaced support girders that had been bolted and anchored into the floor.

Two box trucks about the size of a typical U-Haul were

parked at random angles facing toward the interior of the building.

*Amateurs.*

One of the vehicles had a long scorch mark along its left side. The blackened soot looked strangely artistic on the yellow surface. Boxes were stacked at varying heights around the revelers. The ones nearest the burned truck had been arranged into a recognizable but thoroughly unanticipated shape—a throne.

A pirate, who had clearly been influenced by the Disney films—right down to the scraggly facial hair and raggedy hat—sprawled on the surface. Diana blinked to clear her eyes, but he was still there. "Do you see this, or am I finally having that breakdown I've expected?"

Tony snorted. "If you're referring to the Jack Sparrow wannabe, I see him, too."

Cara chuckled. "I love this job. Every day is a new adventure."

"Yeah. In stupidity," he countered.

Diana couldn't argue the point. "Okay, it's probably safe to assume that pretty boy there is one of our magic users. Be on the lookout for any others." She stuck her head around for another quick glance at the room. This time, she saw a group of women scantily-clad in nightclub attire fawning on either side of the would-be rogue. "We may have some civilians present. Those ladies don't look like they spent their evening robbing liquor stores."

Kayleigh's voice preempted any other responses. "I've taken the feeds from your glasses and run facial recognition. We have nothing on the women, and no additional bounties are present. The ones we knew of are magicals, but we still have no clear indication as to what their powers are. This is the second time they've been seen together. The first was when they made an identical heist on the west side of the city."

Diana checked to be sure her decoy bracelets were in place. "Well, let's make it the last time. Take out the trash, then the buccaneer. Give us a ten-second countdown. We go on zero." The numbers popped into the lower right of her display. She breathed once and braced herself until the count ended.

Shouting and scrambling accompanied their forced entrance on all sides. It might have been inspired in part by Tony's heavy shotgun, which discharged giant beanbags with deafening bangs that echoed in the tumult. It also might have been caused by Cara's battle cry as she leapt from the low platform she'd entered on to land beside a guard with a gun. A well-placed kick knocked his weapon aside, and she took him out of the fight with two squeezes of the trigger from her taser, followed by a sharp kick to the head.

Diana preferred to think her own entry engendered the most chaos. She swept an arm wide to generate a wave of force that crashed over everyone in front of her. As a result, several targets lost their footing, while others were propelled into each other before they slumped in a daze on the floor. As she suspected, the power of the spell wavered and ultimately died before it reached the most important target.

The pirate waved a wand negligently and muttered a word under his breath. He smirked as he rose from his pretentious throne. Silence fell as he shouted, "Hold!" He grinned at Diana and channeled the character with whom he clearly had a deeply dysfunctional para-social relationship, including the accent. "How dare you attack my crew without provocation?"

Diana scowled at him. "Robbing three liquor stores and burning them down is sufficient provocation, scumbag."

"Plunder."

"What?"

"We do not rob," he said solemnly. "We plunder." He struck a dramatic pose. "You stand before the Prince of Plunder. Bow, strumpet."

Her brain went into a vapor lock as she gaped in utter disbelief at the sheer stupidity and arrogance the man demonstrated. His only reply was to raise his ridiculously pointed beard a little higher. She shook her head. "You know what? Let's discuss it after."

The aspiring prince frowned. "After?"

She thrust both hands toward him, used the left to gently guide the half-dressed "strumpet" on that side away from him, and directed a blast of force at him with the other. He twisted with a grace and agility that belied his previous mannerisms and brought his wand up in an arc. The blade of translucent energy that extended from it intercepted her attack and redirected it to collide with a stack of liquor crates partway across the room. The contents shattered and spread the liquid in a geyser of alcohol, followed by a low burble that dripped down the remains to form a pool on the cement floor.

Diana yelled and charged. The world slowed in a manner to which she had become accustomed when dealing with combative magics. Her danger sense had been a lifesaver on more than one occasion, and it still served her well. However, on previous occasions, the power had only allowed time to slow. This time, her view of the situation expanded beyond her normal frame of vision. She saw Tony at a diagonal angle to her left. Cara was almost directly behind her, and yet she could see the former soldier clearly.

The detective swung his shotgun barrel down inch by inch to target the first thug that attacked him. Given the criminal's size, he probably had a Kilomea somewhere in his family tree. She watched the beanbag leave the weapon in its inevitable trajectory toward the hulking form's head.

Cara was a blur, even in slow motion, as she launched a double punch in one direction and a kick in the other. A single leg planted firmly to support her weight as she struck. The reaction against the kick added power to the punch, and both enemies looked primed to take flight the moment time resumed its normal flow.

Diana refocused on the Pirate Prince ahead of her. He held his force blade across his chest in a guard position, ready to intercept any attack she threw. That didn't seem overly concerning. Nothing else stood out to her, so the danger had to emanate from the wand in the hand that currently swung slowly toward her. She twisted away and slid out of its path to avoid all but the edge of the sonic assault he cast at her.

*Sound? What the hell?*

Even the near miss pushed her earpieces into complete defensive silence, and the windows at the end of the shrieking cone shattered explosively outward to let the sun stream in freely. Were she not in the middle of combat, she might even have called the effect charming as the shards spun slowly in their descent.

Everything accelerated again as she completed her rotation. She released another barrage of force blasts at her opponent, but he deflected them with ease. Her telekinesis failed to steal the second wand, and Diana growled at the increasing unreliability of the move which had once been her go-to. Still, the effort allowed her to get close, so it wasn't completely worthless. The pirate fired a second sonic attack, and she conjured a buckler from the force of her will to block the physical power behind the attack, while her earpieces took care of the rest. Next, she parried the blow of the sword construct the pirate had materialized with his first wand.

She popped his knee with a light telekinetic push that jarred his leg and threw his balance off. The opening was small, but it was enough to land a punch if she was quick enough. She wrapped her fist in a force blast that detonated as it struck, and the buccaneer careened backward into a swarm of henchmen who came running to his aid. They fell like so many bowling pins and a smile played on her lips.

*Strike, scumbags.*

Tony and Cara arrived soon after and joined her in victory. A quick glance confirmed the unconscious and broken criminals the partners had left in their wake.

The pirate pushed himself up with a groan and rose to his feet. "Nice hit, lassie."

Diana looked at the woman beside her. "Did he call me a dog?"

Cara snorted. "Technically, he called you a bitch.

Which, to be fair, is probably better than when he called you a whore earlier."

"Strumpet means prostitute?"

Tony nodded, and Diana turned to the pirate with a scowl.

"Did you really call me both a whore and a bitch?"

He shook his head. "That's not exactly how I meant it but…well, if the boot fits…" He raised his hands in an offensive stance, then spun and ran through an opening between the boxes beside him. The BAM agents sprinted in pursuit, only to skid to a stop as another mass of foes materialized between them and their quarry.

Cara cracked her knuckles. "I wondered where the rest of these newbs were hiding."

"Newbs?" Tony asked.

Cara's voice was incredulous. "Newbs. Newbies. Like, new video game players." The former detective didn't fill the expectant pause. "Geez, Tony, how ancient are you?"

Diana laughed.

*I love my team. Even the ancient members.*

"Rath, bad guy on his way out. Fancy hat. Interesting clothes. He's all yours." She rolled her neck and grinned at the enemies facing them. "We have to take out more trash."

# CHAPTER TWO

Rath and Max crouched in the tall grass near the exit route, as planned. The trap wasn't intentional, but it helped to have contingencies in mind in the event of an ineffective takedown.

*Things never go perfectly. Wouldn't be any fun if they did.*

Over the tiny headset he wore, he quoted, "I shall call him Squishy, and he shall be mine." Laughter mingled with the cries of pain that emanated from the fight on the other end of the comms.

Kayleigh and Diana had rigged a carrying harness for Max's field adventures. Rath rode in his customary position at the dog's collar, which had been given additional rings to grasp for stability. There were even a couple of footholds that had been stitched into the weave in case he needed them. The Borzoi wore a set of linked straps on his back that contained the troll's batons, a pair of pepper grenades, and the larger version of his headset. They still hadn't solved the problem of transporting gear for his largest form, nor of making good defensive equipment for his smallest size.

Offense was another matter, though. Rath had a new weapon to try out today. Emerson had rebuilt his needles and inserted a small carbon fiber cylinder into the center. A metal vial threaded into the base of the grip to feed the device. The one he would draw with his right held a sedative toxin, and the other contained pure capsaicin, which would make any being unhappy if they were scratched with it, especially if that scratch happened in a sensitive area.

Three loud bangs resounded as metal slammed against metal like a heavy drum. "A group left out the right side. Three different doors," Kayleigh reported.

Rath frowned. They had only identified a single exit at the center of the building, near where he and Max laid in wait. It would be irritating if the person with the hat came out of another. This bore further investigation.

*Here, Squishy.*

"Max, up half." The dog rose slightly to allow him a view over the top of the long grass. His purple hair would look much like a weed's flower blossoming. He chuckled to himself as the thought settled in.

*Trollflower.*

He scanned the area and confirmed Kayleigh's findings. Many frightened people spewed out two doors on the far sides of the warehouse wall that hadn't initially shown up on the drone's camera. It was likely that an illusion or glamour of some sort had been used to conceal them. The sound of curses and selfish exhortations that echoed from the newly revealed entrances confirmed that others had yet to come. A few vehicles rested in the worn patches of dirt and grass. Their tires had done an exceptional job at trampling the vegetation and revealing the minefield of potholes that lay beneath. A few piles of old equipment rusted in disarray and tripped some of the men in their flight. Rath chuckled.

A cluster of enemies emerged together from the main exit in a tight formation. The troll recognized the signs of an escort from all the movies he'd watched as he'd studied the culture and language of Earth. He risked a single hop above his cover for a better look.

He smiled and whispered, "Drink up, me hearties, yo ho." Then, he leaned down and spoke his instructions quietly. "Max, the one in the middle. Charge, then run away. Don't stop." The Borzoi dipped his long nose in acknowledgment and rose to his full height. A shudder went through him as he shook softly to warm up his muscles before they hurtled forward.

Rath loved every second of riding the dog, regardless of the reason. The world turned into a great colored blur as the breeze generated by his companion's gait blew past his ears. Max wove through the legs of the nearest targets before they had time to react. The men yelled, and the dog's paws scrabbled as he switched directions to find a new gap to exploit.

The troll used their momentum to leap forward in an arced trajectory. He landed cleanly on the man's long coat and scrambled up, using the creases in the heavy fabric as stairs, footholds, and handholds. He tuned out the shouts of dismay and the jostling that surrounded him. Max had done well as a distraction, but now, it was up to him to fulfill his part. He reached the pirate's shoulder and considered going for his favorite target, but the enemy's eardrum was a longer climb and the blood vessels in his neck were inches away. Rath drew the needles from his back and stabbed the one in his right hand into his foe's flesh. With a wide grin, he pushed the injection button and administered the sedative.

Emerson had promised that it would be fast-acting. The man stumbled after only two steps before he began to fall. As the pirate toppled, Rath leapt onto the nearest henchman and clutched his long beard and used it to swing across the front of the man's body and up toward his face. The left-hand spike licked out and drew a line of red down his foe's cheek. The man screamed as the brutal pepper extract seeped into the wound, and the diminutive assailant jumped clear with a wicked laugh.

When he landed, he found himself in the middle of a circle of extended wands. *Uh-oh.* He dashed right, then left, but they tracked his movement. Concentrated force blasts peppered the ground without touching their pirate leader. The narrow space for evasion left the troll with only one option. He launched upward and grew. By the time he reached three feet, he'd landed again. His strong legs propelled him into a two-footed kick that struck the chest of his nearest foe. He tensed and used the surface as a platform to launch at his next target. The guards were taken by surprise, and the tighter quarters made it more difficult to use their attacks without harming one another. This proved to be the case when Rath clawed at his latest opponent's shirt and used it to flip over the man's head to avoid an incoming attack.

The troll dropped to the ground and rolled to dodge the falling body. The scent of burning flesh and smoke was followed by the sight of a hole seared in the dead man's chest. He would have chuckled at the inadvertent pun were he not so occupied with staying alive and dealing with the new use of lethal force.

*Okay, done playing, then.*

He whistled for Max and sprinted to where he'd last seen the dog. The Borzoi erupted from hiding and adjusted his angle to run directly at him. He yelled, "Max, straight draw." They had practiced many options for getting his supplies to him, and this one was the fastest and most reliable. It left him without his headset, but battles weren't for talking, anyway.

He pushed into a somersault over the canine. His hands found the hilts of his batons while he was upside down, and they flicked to full extension as he landed. He slid, turned, and rocketed back toward the men. They had been caught off guard by his move and the sudden death of their comrade at their own hands, but that didn't last long. The troll wove between cones of fire, bounded over spikes of ice, and spun aside to avoid force blasts. The last was the most difficult, given that the attack wasn't visible until it struck, but training with Diana had given him a sense of how the power worked and its general range. The men also weren't prepared to deal with his speed and failed to adjust to his evasions.

*Idiots. Should train more.*

The criminals from the other doors gathered in a group closer to the building, and a smaller number had interposed themselves between the troll and the car the henchmen currently shoved their fallen leader into. The sound of his head striking the metal as they fought to shove him inside made Rath smile, but the giant man who stepped in front to block his view erased it. He held a large knife in his left hand and a wand in his right. The wizard initiated his attack with a force blast and his target spun to avoid it.

This enemy was smarter and followed up with a strong kick. The troll took the blow on a shoulder and continued the spin to burn off momentum. He rolled to complete the maneuver. A boot stomped behind his head, and he forced himself to change direction and roll back toward it. The knife scraped as it dug into the earth, and Rath swallowed. If he hadn't changed course, that blade would have pierced him instead. He flipped to his feet and swept his batons up in a rising cross. It deflected the man's incoming punch, but the low force blast that followed threw him back, knocked his legs from beneath him, and dropped him on his face.

He tasted blood from his bitten lip, and a line on his leg burned like he'd been cut. Mostly, though, he was upset at his failure to guard against the magical attack.

*Must practice with Diana more.*

He rose, lunged at the man, and dodged the ranged attacks with subtle weaves. He feinted a leap, and his foe summoned a force shield to defend himself. Rath grinned and slid low to jam his batons into the man's feet. The shock discharged with a loud snap, and his opponent tottered back and stumbled to one knee. The troll scuttled forward and rammed the tips of his batons into his adversary's chest. This time, the wizard fell as the current disrupted his muscles. Rath shocked him a third time for good measure, then knocked him out with a heavy boot.

By now, the other lackeys had returned to the battle. Once more, the troll evaded force bolts and gouts of flame. He rolled to avoid the onslaught and ran after the dust cloud that marked the car with the pirate in it. His size increased with each step until his growth stopped a little above seven feet. Max barked enthusiastically, and he waved as the dog followed as fast as he could run.

The vehicle had to move slowly as it navigated the pockmarked yard. Too many misadventures in the potholes could easily break an axle or cause some other form of car trouble. This proved advantageous to Rath, albeit somewhat difficult with the various attacks still launched from behind. Whenever an attack was imminent, Max would bark a warning and Rath would react accordingly. Acrobatics were ill-advised in this setting and more difficult in his largest form. It left him far too vulnerable to a force blast, so he settled on rolling or somersaulting instead.

The troll angled toward the left and sprinted at his top speed to cut off their escape at the exit gate. He barely managed to reach the dilapidated security booth in time. Once he was within range of the vehicle, he tensed his legs and vaulted forward to plant his feet solidly on the roof. His increased weight buckled the metal, and he struck at the windshield with both fists. The laminated safety glass spidered with obscuring cracks. He sneered as he raised his fists for another blow.

One of the pirate's flunkies leaned out the window with a twin set of pistols in both hands. Rath calculated the angles and flung himself aside as the bullets whined past him, and he tumbled through the dirt on the side of the car opposite the gunner. He growled at the departing vehicle and shook his fist once before he loped toward the building.

The rest of the team was outside, wrapping up the fallen bounties. They had undertaken this operation both for setup funds and to get useful information. The former, at least, was covered. As for the latter, he doubted that the man in the costume had much intelligence to give, even if they had managed to capture him. He turned to stare down the road in the direction in which the car had vanished.

*Stupid Squishy. When we meet again, your hat is mine.*

# CHAPTER THREE

The restaurant was one she'd wanted to try for some time but hadn't had the opportunity for the trip to the suburbs to do so until now.

*Busy, busy, busy. And there are so many great places in town.*

The fact that Cara and Tony had been in the area marketing the security agency provided the needed excuse for the gathering, and she was in a good mood as she pulled the doors open.

*Plus, finding our missing shipment of anti-magic bullets in the warehouse was a huge bonus.*

The inside was appropriately dark and filled with twinkling lights, skeletons, and other paraphernalia celebrating Dia de Los Muertos. Rumor had it that the burritos were excellent and the beer selection formidable, which had been enough to put it high on her list. Rath trailed a step behind her as Diana entered and offered a "Whoa" of astonishment.

If the host was surprised to see a three-foot tall purple-haired troll enter the establishment, he didn't show it. "Your party is in the back." She took a moment to wonder how he knew, then realized that Rath was probably a good way to identify her.

*Yet another reason to keep him on the periphery of bounty runs when we can.*

Rath slid in beside Cara, and Diana followed. They placed drink orders, and the server bustled away. There was already a mountain of tortilla chips surrounded by several kinds of salsa in the center of the half-circular table, and they dug in. Rath amused himself by building teetering structures out of the chips while the rest chatted.

Diana grinned at Tony. "So, how'd we do?"

He finished chewing and took a casual sip to enable his speech. "You timed that when my mouth was full on purpose. Petty, boss. Real petty." He shook his head. "Anyway, we did well. Most had bounties. A couple were randoms mixed up with them, but they'll go down, too. We found most of the liquor, although it looks like some was moved before we got there."

Cara threw a chip at him. "Or the local PD picked up a few bottles here or there, right, Detective?"

He grinned. "The spoils of war. And don't tell me it didn't happen now and again in the Marshalls, too." He turned to Diana with a neutral expression. "Even if we consider that such things might have happened, there was still enough missing to suggest it went elsewhere."

Rath grumbled, "Maybe to pirate boat."

The others laughed, and Cara replied, "Right. How about that outfit? Did anyone notice a schooner or galleon sailing up the Monongahela yesterday? It seems like it would've been hard to miss."

Diana had to make a difficult admission. "I rather liked the look. Well, the boots, actually. But at least he's trying." Her teammates stared at her in a way that suggested they doubted her sanity.

The troll regarded her with suspicious eyes. "Dibs on the hat." That set off another round of laughter, which was quickly interrupted by the arrival of their drinks and the need to order food other than chips.

When the waiter left, Tony resumed his report. "A couple of the extras acquired bounties after the fact, thanks to some clever paperwork wrangling, so we actually picked up more than we expected. In short, we're golden to expand the labs. Speaking of which, where's Kayleigh?"

She sighed. "Living in denial about remaining in Pittsburgh. She's spending the weekend in DC." Cara coughed and her boss pointed a finger at her. "Don't say it. She's staying."

The other woman shook her head as she tried and failed to smother her grin. "Chip. Choking." Diana scowled, and the ex-Marshall took a hasty sip.

Tony came to her rescue. "Well, in any case, we'll need the lab gear, regardless of who uses it, and the cash flow means we can hire both new agents without worry, right?"

Diana nodded. "Yep, it does. So, the big question is who should we recruit first?" The team had discussed that issue from every possible perspective. In the three weeks since the events at the Cube, they'd worked hard to find information on the Remembrance—and failed more often than they'd succeeded—which shifted the balance toward an undercover expert. But it was impossible to deny that having a demolitions professional on hand might have changed the explosive outcome of that evening.

*Decisions, decisions.*

Naturally, the argument began again. Tony, ever the investigator, immediately answered, "Face. We need the intel."

Cara countered, "Demo, because bad guys with explosives suck."

"Don't mess with the demolition man," Rath added, which really could be read either way.

Diana had asked Bryant for his opinion, but the smart-aleck simply texted three words.

**You're the boss.**

She grimaced at the memory.

*Helpful. Chucklehead.*

But the weeks of floundering for information had taken their toll. She didn't like being in the dark this long. That landed her solidly in the intel-gathering camp. "Tony has a valid point. We need data on both sides of the house, so Face it is." He cheered, Cara groaned, and Rath continued to stack chips with a small grin.

Their food arrived, and they spent time debating the values of tacos vs. soft tacos vs. burritos. Diana believed in all three but had requested a carnitas burrito that turned out to be phenomenal. Rath had ordered a quesadilla and seemed to enjoy the stretchy cheese that filled it. His gleeful grin pulled her tired cheeks into a mirrored response.

*He always makes me smile.*

As if reading her mind, the troll gazed up at that moment with a piece of quesadilla held in his teeth. A trail of yellow string connected it to the plate below. That did it for her. She laughed out loud, and the others soon joined in.

Diana paused as she remembered something. "We need to be on the lookout for a magic tech, too. Kayleigh said that she—and whoever replaces her—would stick to the practical rather than the magical since we have a supply hookup in the Kemana. Ideally, we want one who can play cyber wizard, too."

Tony laughed. "I would also like a unicorn, please."

She nodded. "Right? But hey, it's worth a look." She looked at Rath. "What do you lack, young padawan?"

The troll put down the bite he was about to take and grinned. "Lightsaber would be good."

Diana smiled at the joke.

"Sleep and pepper poisons are great. Saddle is great. Need knives for training."

She nodded again, this time with a frown. "Seriously, why do so many of these jerks have blades?"

Cara replied as she counted on her fingers. "Easy to get, easy to hide, easy to use."

Tony sighed. "All right, let's get serious. What can we do to keep Kayleigh here?"

"All I can think of is to get her more stuff." Diana shrugged. "I've told her to hire an assistant, but she doesn't want to do it since she 'won't be staying.' Honestly, she's the most stubborn person I know." She saw their stares and shrugged. "Okay, most stubborn person other than me."

More laughter followed. "So, boss, how do we operationalize all this?" Tony asked.

Diana delayed her response with a few bites while she considered the question. "First, we need to interview the Face. That's on you two. Figure it out and make it happen. Fly wherever you have to. Then we'll gear the lab up. I'll put Kayleigh on it and tell her it should be her dream workspace. That ought to get her moving."

She turned to Rath. "You and I will buy practice knives. There's a martial arts place in the strip district that should have a decent selection." The troll nodded. Her phone vibrated, and she sighed. "Okay, buddy, we'll have to do that the day after tomorrow. It seems I have plans starting at sunrise. I've been summoned to Stonehaven."

Cara asked, "The lady?" They all enjoyed visiting with the elf in charge of the Kemana under the city.

"Worse. Nylotte. Class is back in session."

The other woman actually growled at the woman's name. "Much worse. She's..." She struggled to find the words. Finally, she ground out an exaggerated, "Awful."

Diana nodded with a grim chuckle.

Rath sounded approving as he said, "Diana. Fighting Mode. Must Train. Is Good."

"Yeah, that. Is good." In truth, she didn't completely hate the training sessions. They were a little heavy on the pain at times, but the healing potions always took care of the damage eventually. And the Drow had proven to be a reliable source of information on all things uncanny. Still, not getting a magical beatdown every few days would also be nice.

She looked around the table at the people who trusted

her to lead them, as well as the troll who had adopted her. It occurred to her, not for the first time, that they were a family.

*And I can endure anything for however long I have to in order to protect them, even Nylotte.*

# CHAPTER FOUR

Diana strode along the now-familiar streets of Kemana Stonehaven. She still traveled the main street whenever possible and gazed with frank longing at the boots, clothes, and blades in the various shops. She hadn't convinced Kayleigh to join her yet but thought the tech could do wonderful things with the materials they used in the district to create her next pair of spy bot prototypes. The purple crystals on the cavern roof bathed the place in a peculiar and literally unearthly glow that set her mind at ease. The strange construction materials and odd styling were recognizable after all the time she'd spent in the underground city and gave her a strange sense of comfort.

*If I keep visiting, it'll feel as much like home as Pittsburgh does.*

She took the small path that led to the darker street that ran parallel to the main road and walked briskly to Nylotte's shop. The other storekeepers had warmed to her presence enough that they no longer slammed the doors of their shops when she was near, but that was the limit of their welcome. Whether it was prejudice against her humanity, a dislike of her connection to the acerbic Drow, or something more, Diana had no idea. She didn't really care either. There was no room in her brain to worry about anything else. She had reached maximum concern capacity.

Today, she'd dressed entirely in black, except for her jacket. Her jeans fell over the hidden knives and revolver in her boots, and she wore a wide belt with a vintage Ziggy Stardust buckle over a tucked-in tank top. One of her favorite leather racing jackets finished the look and added a splash of color with a yellow stripe down its left side.

Nylotte was waiting when Diana came through the door and took the lead as they descended the long staircase to the basement. The stairs made three right-angle turns on the way down. The cellar was fully the size of the shop above and was broken into sections. Two-thirds of the space was devoted to a large training area with metal rings inlaid on the floor to set boundaries for the combat zone. The remaining third was stacked with crated goods and held a workspace where the Drow presumably worked with artifacts and created potions, based on the items for sale upstairs. She'd never explained and Diana hadn't asked, mainly because of the capacity problem. Her teacher already occupied a not insubstantial portion of her worrying energy.

The sessions always began with a version of the pushing hands game they had played on the day of her first assessment. Nylotte would call out the magic she was about to use, and Diana would defend herself with the same variety, if possible, or with a different form if she was unable. So far, she'd been electrified, burned, crushed, and had her flesh and spirit scoured by shadows. The Drow seemed in total control at all times and stopped before inspiring true dread of impending demise.

*Most of the time, anyway.*

She hung her leather jacket on a protected hook in the work area and took position across from her teacher in silence. After a moment, she broke their ritual by raising a hand to sketch the Elven rune for question. As an added portion to her training, she had requested to learn the spoken, written, and gestural forms of the language. The skills came slowly, but she felt it was important as a way to connect to her heritage. When she'd told Nylotte this, the woman had only smiled and changed the subject. Now, she nodded to grant her student permission to speak. "Someone tried to blast me with sound a couple of days ago."

The dark elf laughed with a joy that seemed out of place. "You've met the self-proclaimed prince, then."

She frowned. "Yes. How did you know that so quickly?"

When happy, Nylotte's face wasn't very different from her normal visage. Sharp lines, pretty lips, and smooth skin defined her features and obscured her true age. A shock of white hair fell long and full down her back, like the crest of a wave over a dark shore. It was the Drow's eyes that gave it away, though. A certain sparkle betrayed the mirth within. "It is a rare choice, quite impractical for use on a small scale. If you wish to break off part of a cliff or collapse a cave, sonic magic is an excellent option. It's not particularly controllable for anything less ambitious."

Diana could think of a lot of potential uses but had learned quickly not to argue with her teacher unless it was truly essential. "So why does he use it?"

The woman laughed again.

*So weird.*

"He would say it's all about panache."

"Panache."

"Yes."

"So, he's fond of alliteration."

"And presenting a polished pose. And performing punchy prose."

"Stop."

"If that's what you positively prefer, protege."

Diana groaned and prepared herself for combat.

*This is probably what she's like when she's drunk. I hope she doesn't kill me.*

"I'm ready, teacher."

Nylotte nodded and glided into her attacking stance. Her leather pants hugged tightly to her legs, and her high boots still inspired deep envy in her apprentice. She wore an odd top that buttoned left of center from neck to mid-thigh and was adorned with black embroidery on the scarlet fabric. It looked Chinese and added an extra martial edge to her overall appearance.

The Drow attacked first with force, a battering line that Diana deflected with a shield scarcely larger than her fist. She was prohibited from counterattacking, but her mind cataloged the options and she wondered if there was a way to reflect the energy back at her mentor. Power surged within her, and the blocker shifted from a small curved circle to a larger concave oval. The next blast bounced off it with barely an impact and rebounded.

Her teacher's dark eyes widened slightly, and she swept the bolt away with a negligent wave. "Interesting."

Diana lost focus in her shock at the unexpected magic. The next force bolt struck her before she could raise a defense, and she cursed as it punched her in the chest. Hastily, she blocked the one that followed with the normal shield. She thought about reflection again, but no power surge materialized, and her construct remained the same. When Nylotte switched to lightning, she tried to summon her own and pictured a defensive oval surrounding her whole body. Despite her attempt, she was soon wreathed in electricity, but not her own. Inevitably, she fell and gritted her teeth to suppress her groans as the Drow's attack licked and bit at her before it fell away.

She stumbled quickly to her feet. Day one had taught her that to remain on the ground any longer than absolutely necessary led to a resumption of the assault. Her teacher said, "Fire," and Diana focused her mind to seek inside for flame. Despite the instinctive visualization of her power as a molten pool, she couldn't yet draw it forth in that form. When the attack came, she pushed down her panic and summoned a force barrier to protect herself. She extended the wall toward her opponent with an effort of will, a new strategy she'd developed in consultation with Cara. The blazing cone was deflected in all directions but remained within the magical boundary set by the outer circle. The kind of ritual magic that made such a thing possible was as far beyond her as calculus was to a sloth, assuming the creature would wake up long enough to consider it.

The agent actually felt the slightest edge of pride in her abilities before Nylotte blasted it away. Shadow tentacles squirmed across the floor toward her, and she panicked. Her shield dropped, and she rolled to avoid the fire that still sought her. She spun to her feet, ready to fight, but the other woman had abandoned the attacks. Diana growled. "That was a dirty trick."

The Drow laughed. "You started it. That was a good strategy, but it blocked your view of me."

The anger evaporated when she realized that A, she was right, and B, that was incredibly stupid.

*Why does she always have to be right?*

She swallowed her pride for what seemed like the hundredth time in the weeks they'd trained together. "You're right. That wasn't smart."

"That is why we practice. However, it is obvious that additional combat instruction is not a good idea today. Your emotions are too close to the edge."

Diana sighed. As usual, the other woman's vision pierced to her core. "True."

Nylotte gestured at the side of the ring and a pair of oversized red and black cushions spun into place at the center of the circle. She lowered herself to the closer of the two, and her trainee sat on the one opposite, crossing her legs in a less graceful imitation of her teacher.

The Drow's voice lacked its usual edge of sarcasm when she spoke this time. "I would like to try something new today. However, it will require great trust on your part. More than you have previously given."

Diana tried to moderate her expression and managed to transform the scowl into a slight frown by the time it reached her face. "What did you have in mind?"

The Dark Elf chuckled, but joy had been replaced by earnest gravity. "That's an interesting choice of words because your mind is the answer."

She suppressed a flinch at the idea. "You're talking about something more than reading my thoughts if you're this serious about it."

Nylotte nodded. "Yes. I'm asking you to let me into it."

"I don't even understand how that's possible."

"I know, and it's okay." The other woman chuckled. "I need to lead you to a greater understanding of your magic. But there are things that you cannot be told, only shown, and I am unable to guide you without seeing them for myself. So, as your teacher and one who wishes to help you achieve progress, I am asking you to lower your barriers and let me in."

Diana frowned. "You can't do it yourself?"

The Drow folded her arms and tapped a nail against her arm. Diana knew that annoyed tap very well. "Yes. I could, but it would damage you, potentially beyond repair."

"Oh. Okay. That would be bad." Her mind bucked instinctively at the idea.

*It's messy in there. Seriously, I haven't cleaned...ever.*

She put her face in her hands and pressed her palms against her eyes until it was fully dark, then tried to reason her way through it.

*Okay. She's basically able to kill me at any time. We both know this. Why does this worry me so much?*

*What if this is like body-snatching and she takes you over?* mental Diana replied.

Dread washed over her at the idea.

*But she's shown no such inclination. Plus, it's not like I'm particularly special. She's already far more powerful than me. And our security protocols would identify anyone who was...in me but wasn't me.*

*She* could practically see her suspicious self shake its head.

*You're an idiot. Do you know that?*

*And when has that stopped me before?*

She broke into an unexpected grin and opened her eyes to find her mentor watching her with narrowed eyes. "Okay, let's do it."

# CHAPTER FIVE

Nylotte brought out a formal crockery service on a tray, and Diana experienced a surreal moment when she realized that the Dark Elf was performing a very traditional Japanese tea ceremony. It made the woman seem more serious about her craft than she had given her credit for. It also made her more concerned about what was to come.

*I hope this isn't my final cup of tea for, like, ever.*

*I did warn you.*

*Shut up, me.*

The Drow finished swishing the bamboo stirrer and offered a bowl to Diana. She accepted it and breathed in the aroma that carried hints of chamomile, cardamom, and several other scents she couldn't identify. Still a little cautious, she sipped carefully and was surprised to find the blend delicious. She took another sip, and her mind began to swim.

Nylotte smiled and she raised her head. "This brew should never be shared with anyone you don't trust as it removes resistances of all kinds." She put a lascivious purr in the last words, and Diana laughed. The humor brought a picture to her of a double date, her and Bryant with Nylotte and someone, and she snorted again at her inner critic's opinion of that concept.

"Clearly, the drink has done its work." Her teacher set the tea aside. "It will be easier to cross the barriers we need to." She took her trainee's hands in her own and guided their arms to rest on their knees. The soft warmth of her flesh was so different from her sharp appearance, and the smooth skin of her palms left Diana wondering how she had survived in a cutthroat world without losing that beauty.

*Okay, that's weird. I'm clearly a little drunker than I thought.*

The soft voice was almost a caress. "This always seems strange the first time. Later, you will learn to use the technique to build your reserves. For now, stay with me. Focus on my words."

Power trickled through their physical connection and climbed Diana's arms. When it reached her head, the swirl in her brain increased and her vision clouded. The mists receded and the room was no longer present. Instead, they stood in a forest clearing and a dry fog obscured the ground. A raised stone table stood before them, and she looked passively at her own recumbent body.

The Drow gestured, and lines glowed on the surface of the figure. Each was slightly translucent and varied in color. They wove through the traditional Chakra points she had seen on late-night television commercials any number of times. She laughed.

*No, that was a giggle.*

*Shut up, inner voice. You're no fun.*

"Are we here to learn Reiki? Like a correspondence course?"

The Drow grinned. "You're entertaining when you're not so tightly clenched. But no, no massage today. These are the paths of power in the body. You can see that each flows through one or more nexuses. A problem in those locations often indicates blocked magic. You may have an issue somewhere that closes you off from your full potential."

Diana's smile transformed into a frown. "So, we'll fix it?"

Nylotte's hair flowed strangely as she shook her head. It was as though gravity had less authority in the liminal space. "That is beyond today's efforts. You will need to be much more skilled to manage that. But if a blockage exists, we may one day be able to clear it. Today, we shall limit ourselves to understanding." She gestured again, and the white line that intersected the highest Chakra intensified. Both the thread and the nexus appeared to be constructed of faceted crystal, and power pulsed within them.

The elf traced a fingertip along a crevice on her student's palm, and the ivory path on her virtual body pulsed again. "What we're looking at is your telekinesis. As you can see, it is unblocked but also isolated." Diana followed the trail and noted that it crossed no other lines and intersected with no other Chakra points. "This makes that skill dependable and easily called upon, but not as powerful as it would be if you could add other energy."

She leaned forward to peer more closely at the Crown Chakra. "So, more intersections, more potential?"

"In part." Nylotte nodded. "Additional overlaps with other lines also provide a way for power to travel to that talent."

"Is there anything I can do to increase a particular ability?"

"Not at your current skill level, and likely not without making sacrifices in other areas. Nature doesn't want us to possess unlimited capacity, or she would have designed us differently." Her teacher waved, and a second line illuminated, more impure than the other. It shimmered blue but was less crystalline and vibrant. Its top loop extended near the Crown Chakra but didn't quite reach it. Instead, it intersected the Third Eye Chakra and flowed out toward her hands, where the path met one other on each side. "This is your force talent."

"What are those that it crosses?"

The Drow illuminated them to reveal a uniform brown that intersected with a lower point. "Unknown. Another kind of magic, certainly."

"So everyone has the potential to do everything, as long as they have magic in the first place?"

Her teacher shook her head before she'd finished the sentence. "The pathways are present, but an individuals' ability to access them is dependent upon their own natures. There are no absolutes." She pointed out the rest of the lines, which overlapped one another and her force power. "When you use magic in the unconscious fashion you've described to me, the energy from somewhere jumps paths without your direction. That is...unusual, to say the least."

"So most magic users can control that?"

"Most magic users lack the potential to do so, intentionally or otherwise. As I've said, you are a rare specimen." The intonation on the last word conjured the image of a frog in a jar.

"How do we find out what the others do?"

Nylotte sighed and released her hands, and the image fell away. Diana blinked as her vision returned. "We wait until something manifests and go in to discover what has changed. Were you weaker in power, I could remain in your mind and help you map them by trial and error. But to do so in our current states of power would be dangerous to both of us—probably fatally so, given your abilities."

Her hopes vanished like they'd been sucked from the world, which reminded her of the request she'd talked herself into earlier as she walked through the Kemana. "I need to know how to create a portal."

The Drow raised an elegant eyebrow. "We can attempt this, but it's dangerous, for many reasons."

"Like teleporting into a solid object kind of dangerous?"

She nodded. "Possibly. But more perilous is the portal that goes awry and rips the veil between this realm and the World in Between."

Diana frowned. "Is it mostly colorless, dark, and as scary as hell?"

"That is one way to describe the place, certainly."

"What is it?"

"A hellscape. Eternal purgatory. The land where

demons come from. Damnation. There are many names for it."

"So, basically, don't go there. Ever."

"The World in Between is not a place one enters with hope for return. And if a return occurs, stories describe life afterward as almost always worse than death, for the horrors experienced within change one forever."

"Gotcha. Never screw up the portal."

Her teacher smiled. "Exactly. Now, let's see what you're capable of."

Hours later, she emerged from the shop, having failed yet again to live up to Nylotte's expectations.

*It's probable that no student manages a portal on their first day. She's ridiculous.*

Diana stared at the long walk back to the surface and sighed.

*But the sooner the better. To hell with the job reasons. I'm tired of walking those stairs.*

# CHAPTER SIX

Morning sunlight glittered on the river outside the window as Diana poured a cup of coffee from the pot on the credenza. Cara and Tony were already seated at the interview table, alongside their candidate for undercover investigator, a man by the name of Sloan Woodham. They had moved quickly from making fun of his name when opening his file to wanting him on the team after reading it.

Her team had returned from the initial meeting with him in St. Louis convinced that he was the one, but they'd all agreed that she would need to vet any candidate before an offer could be made. His back was to her, so all she knew so far was that he had long hair with a subtle curl to it.

*It's probably prettier than mine, at this point.*

She'd managed a hasty ponytail after sleeping in. The training with Nylotte sapped both magical and mundane energies, despite the reservoir of power contained in the purple crystals of the Kemana's roof.

In silence, she circled the table to sit beside Tony and stared across at Cara and their candidate. The word **cute** popped into her glasses, which confirmed both Kayleigh's access to the room through the newly installed cameras and her opinion of the newcomer. "Thanks for making the trip. I hope these two have treated you well."

"Definitely." His voice was smooth, much like the rest of his appearance. "I'd heard about the whole fries-and-slaw on the sandwich thing, but to actually experience it was something else entirely. I certainly wasn't ready for breakfast this morning. In fact, I may never eat again." They all laughed. Primanti's was a legend in Pittsburgh, and rightfully so. Rath was a big fan, naturally. "It's a cool place you have here."

"Nice of you to say so. We like it so far. So, tell me about yourself."

His humble shrug didn't quite ring true. "Degree in Criminal Justice. Recruited by the FBI. Spent some time doing normal agent stuff, then went undercover. Domestic terrorist organizations."

*He has the right look for it.*

Sloan was visually perfect—a square jaw, sharp cheekbones, blue eyes, and perfectly styled blond hair. He still had the build of the high school quarterback he'd been.

*And a good one, too, according to the record books.*

"I was ready to head back under when you contacted me."

Diana grinned but kept it as non-aggressive as possible. "That's a perfect rehash of your file. Now, tell us something we don't know."

His laugh was surprisingly deep and cheerful. "Okay, I

can do that. Last year, I was part of this group of good old boys out in the Midwest. They were working toward a fertilizer bomb but weren't able to buy what they needed in bulk, so each of them would go to different stores every day to pick up a few bags."

He scratched the back of his neck and shook his head. "I gotta hand it to them, they were willing to put the work in. Anyway, I passed the word along and the local PD found the evidence they needed. When they came in for the bust, there was a lot of shouting, but it went down easily. Anyway, one female cop was absolutely gorgeous, even under all the armor, and I couldn't help myself. I was cuffed, assumed I was safe, and asked her where she'd been all my life." He laughed. "She fractured my cheekbone with a right hook. Apparently, you do not flirt with the Midwest police."

They chuckled, and he delivered the punch line. "That woman is now my wife." They stared at him in utter disbelief. Finally, Diana slapped her hands on the table and snorted.

"You're good. I almost believed it."

He grinned and nodded. "It's what I do."

"The person who pointed us to you said you had some magic ability. That's a desirable thing in this organization."

He looked a little uncomfortable, and she knew what he felt, having gone through it herself for many years. Still, he didn't pause for long before he spoke. "I can often sense others' emotions and actually hear their thoughts on rare occasions. I can't control either of those, really. They come as flashes of insight. For instance, you were positive toward me as you sat down." She nodded. "I also apparently have really good mental shielding to prevent people from reading me. I don't do anything." He shrugged. "It's a built-in feature."

Tony smoothed his mustache thoughtfully. "That would be beneficial in your line of work."

"Undoubtedly. The FBI folks decided that having these abilities drew me to a job where I could use them."

Cara laughed. "So, it was either undercover cop or Vegas mentalist extraordinaire?"

The smile he gave her was way flirty, in Diana's opinion.

*I wonder if I need to make a policy against fraternization. Actually, I wonder if ARES already has one.*

Bryant came to mind, and she squashed the thought as Sloan resumed his explanation. "I was fairly good at party tricks in college, that's for sure, but the fun evaporated quickly because I couldn't control it. It made asking girls out on dates easier, though, since I usually knew how they'd answer ahead of time." He stared at Cara with a raised eyebrow.

Diana interrupted, "Okay, it sounds like you have some useful skills. We'll have to chat about you behind your back, of course."

They stood and shook hands and Tony asked, "Do you ever use illusions of any kind?"

Sloan shook his head. "I know there are artifacts out there to do it, but I wouldn't trust it on a job. It's too risky. I would consider it while not undercover, probably—hide my good looks, that kind of thing."

Tony and Cara led him from the room, still chatting. Diana tapped her glasses. "What do you think?"

Text popped onto her display.

**Cute. Seems to like Cara. Would fit in well.**

"My thoughts exactly. I bet you could turn his head if you tried."

The next letters came in caps.

**I'M NOT STAYING.**

Diana smothered a grin.

*Oh yes, you are.*

---

They reconvened in the core so Kayleigh could join them in the flesh. The tech wore her AR glasses and smiled at her teammates. "The drone is following the marker we put on his rental car. I'll have to take over in person once he stops."

Cara nodded. "Hopefully, he won't do anything stupid before we can make him an offer."

"Or after," Tony added,

"Why?" The ex-Marshall grinned. Are you afraid he'll muscle in on your exclusive area of doing stupid things?"

The former detective folded his arms. "Funny you should use the word 'muscle.' Was that a Freudian slip?"

Diana laughed as Cara stuck her tongue out at him. "Okay, children, let's focus, shall we? Are we all in agreement that he's our choice?" There were nods all around. "Good. On to the Demolition Man. Or Woman."

Kayleigh gestured at the table between them, and three pictures appeared. "Preliminary research says all of these are viable options, but none are known to have magic." She pointed to the image projected on her left, a dapper man with dark hair and eyes. "Kensington is SAS but holds dual citizenship. He's currently stationed in Manchester." A flick of a wrist scrolled to the next image, an older stocky woman with blonde hair. "Addens is with the LAPD Bomb Squad. She's been there for a decade and a half." The last picture cycled in and doubled in size. "Anik is the nearest. He's with the Virginia State PD Bomb Squad." He was a dark man who clearly had ancestral roots in the Middle East.

Tony clenched his hands into fists and growled "Khaaaaannnnn." The room filled with groans and Cara slapped him on the shoulder. He laughed. "You know, this team needs call signs. Obviously, if Anik joins us, he has to be Khan."

Diana rolled her eyes. "Call signs. Right. On the list, at the bottom. Moving on." She gestured at the images of the potential new agents. "Thoughts?"

The investigator studied the images. "Well, it's currently three women and one man, so it's only reasonable that we add another male to the team."

"Sloan is male," Cara replied dryly.

He laughed. "I didn't think you'd noticed. Okay, that's still three-to-two."

"Rath is male, too," Kayleigh pointed out.

Tony shook his head. "Rath is a troll. That doesn't count unless we want another troll to balance the species in the group."

Diana groaned. "One is enough, thanks."

The tech snapped her fingers. "Bryant is male."

Their boss shook her head. "Bryant identifies only as annoying." They all laughed. "Well, seeing as there's no clear frontrunner, how about we start with the closest? Virginia is only a hop, skip, and a jump away." They nodded. "Good. We can reserve Kensington and Addens for later expansion."

"ARES UK," Tony said. "I like it."

Cara folded her arms and nodded. "Me, too."

"I'm surprised you have any liking left in you. I thought you spent it all on Sloan."

"Tony, stop trying to make funny happen. You lack the skill."

He answered with a gesture that invoked another round of laughter.

---

Rath had seen disorganized spaces before—Diana's room, for one—but Professor Charlotte Stanley's office was in a category all its own. The back wall had two tall windows, both clean and sparkly, that filtered the late morning sun. Her desk sat in front of them and put the woman in silhouette as the light bent around her.

Every other wall was covered in bookshelves, except for the entry door, and every flat surface in the small room was stacked with books, papers, and ancient-looking things of every description. A meandering path led from the entrance to the desk, bound on both sides by more piles of stuff.

It was marvelous.

He had given Max a stern warning not to knock anything over when they entered, and the dog had obligingly found a patch of unstacked floor under one of the room's two visitor chairs. Rath had vaulted onto the desk and sat on a coffee mug the professor had overturned for him. The fact that it featured a picture of a troll appealed to him. Clearly, the professor liked Oriceran things judging by all the foreign items around the room.

She hit a final key with a flourish and said, "Grading complete. Thank you for waiting, Rath."

"No problem."

"So, how have things been? Do you still like your new hometown?"

He nodded. "Yes. Is good. We are the Pittsburgh Law."

Her long crystal earrings bobbed with her nod. "I wondered if the rumors that there was a troll present at that dreadful prison thing were true and if it was you. I assume that's a yes to both?"

"Yep. Not Max, though. Max isn't ready. Still training."

The dog gave a soft, offended growl, then put his head down again. The professor laughed. "Well, perhaps he's simply smart enough not to get involved in exploding buildings."

Rath shrugged. "Maybe. Is great partner, anyway."

"Your loyalty is a mark in your favor, my friend." She gasped. "That's right." She rummaged in her desk and retrieved a pale purple gem. "I found this in a collection of artifacts the University had in storage. Is it what I think it is?"

He took it from her and a tingle spread into his hands as the energy flowed out of it and into him. "Ooh!" He set it down quickly and felt jangly from the magical flow. "Power crystal. From Kemana."

She smiled. "As I thought. Please, take it with you. It's

yours now." The smile thinned a little, and her words were hesitant. "Have you visited a Kemana? I've never been able to manage an invitation to the one below Pittsburgh."

He shook his head. "No. But will soon. Promised."

"Someone in your family has been?"

He nodded.

"Well, when you go, you *must* remember everything about it for me. I've put in a request through the right channels, but I haven't heard from them yet. There's so much to learn. I'm sure..." Her voice trailed off.

"Will."

Charlotte smiled warmly at him. "Thank you, Rath. I can only imagine what kinds of beings might be down there."

He snorted. "Stupid Mirennas, probably."

She blinked, stared at the stacks on her desk with a small frown, and pulled a volume from the middle of the nearest one. A steadying hand on the top of the pile prevented the makeshift Jenga tower from collapsing. She folded the book open to a page near the center and showed him a picture. "Is this what you mean?"

"Yep. Bouncy stupid monkeys."

The professor turned the book toward herself and read out loud. "The Mirenna is one of the more aggressive creatures found in the Dark Forest." Her eyes widened as she looked at him. "That sounds alarming. Did they hurt you?"

"No." He flipped and mimed fighting them with his batons. "We won. Monkeys lost."

She shook her head. "Well, it seems you have things properly under control in your new home. I wondered if you would like to come to my class in a couple of days? I'll do a talk on Oriceran history, naturally, and you might find it interesting. At best, you could share some of your perspectives. I'm sure the students would enjoy seeing a real troll in the flesh."

Rath nodded. "Would love to."

She grinned. "Excellent."

# CHAPTER SEVEN

The portal broke the stillness of the ruined courtyard. The sunlight was cold and cast the area in sharp relief. Dreven had arrived early and walked the path that wound through the broken stones. The ghosts of the structures that had once existed projected themselves from his memory and stately columns rose proudly from the crumbling foundations to circle the fountain the Remembrance used for their meetings. These last vestiges of older times served as voiceless witnesses to their plans.

The witch, Iressa, was next to arrive. She was likewise early, as was their agreement. She walked to his side and flashed him a flawless smile. As always, he felt how easy it would be to surrender to that façade of ravishing beauty and become her plaything. Her black dress hugged her slim curves provocatively and offered a subtle invitation all its own. Again, he marshaled his inner strength against the idea. He considered lashing out in response to her seductive effort, but while it might have been intentional, it could also be the woman's natural state. She'd practiced putting others under her spells, both literal and figurative, for so long that she likely couldn't turn it off.

He chose a simple nod instead. "Thank you for coming. I have come to believe that your ideas offer the best path forward—that we must make a louder statement against the humans and the kemana both."

"Of course I'm right. A child could see that."

The wizard suppressed his annoyance. "Be that as it may, we should act together from here on."

She cocked her head to the side. "Do you believe they will still argue the point?"

"I do. They are more wedded to their perspectives than I am."

Iressa smirked. "I've always admired your flexibility, Dreven."

He managed not to roll his eyes at the tease in her tone. "Excellent. You should get back to your platform. It's almost time." She put an extra sway in her hips as she walked away, and Dreven suppressed a shudder.

*Beautiful but deadly.*

At the appointed moment, the other three portals manifested in their usual places. Iressa was in motion as the first hole in the fabric of reality appeared and doubtless looked as if she had only recently arrived from her own portal.

*Which serves my purposes perfectly.*

When they had all positioned themselves, Dreven gestured with his wand to raise the protective shield around them and block all senses of sight and sound from their gathering. He looked at each of his fellow leaders, then nodded. "As always, first, we must speak of the past. Pesharn, your attack did not go as planned."

The dwarf who stood between him and the Kilomea offered a gruff, "Indeed. Do tell us the details of your failure." As always, the robe and cowl helped to conceal part of his face, but he still clanked with the sound of the armor beneath the soft façade.

The Kilomea stretched to her full height and glared contemptuously at her stubby accuser. "Accessing the prison itself was always a hope, rather than a plan. It is no surprise that the humans protected it adequately, given the power of the individuals they incarcerate within. However, the building they used as a decoy provided a very satisfying explosion."

The dark-skinned gnome at her side added, "Which we took credit for, revealing the Remembrance to the authorities, as planned. My people have spread the word of our existence through the magical communities on Earth, seeking new recruits to join us in future successes. To call it a failure is to overstate the matter, Jarkko." The dwarf nodded in acknowledgment but displayed no sign of regret or responsibility.

Iressa's sultry tones washed over them all, and she extended her hands wide. "Peace, friends. The assault accomplished our intent. That it was far too conservative an effort is not Pesharn's fault. It is all of yours. Ours." It was obvious she didn't believe she shared in that failure. Dreven met her gaze and tilted his head slightly. She smiled and continued, "Now, it is time to think bigger. We must set the stage and bring the curtain down on our enemies with a major strike at the opposition, both above and below the surface."

Their leader nodded. "So, let us speak of the future. What shall we do? I will reserve my own comments for the end." He held a hand out to the dwarf.

Jarkko frowned and folded his burly arms. "Another strike. Bigger. Bolder. And then another after that until our enemies are driven into retreat, where we can crowd them and crush them."

*Surprisingly martial today, aren't we, my friend? Speaking of martial…*

Dreven gestured toward Pesharn.

The Kilomea did not speak for several moments as she pondered the situation. "Our prey is spooked. It may be wise to stalk in the shadows until they lower their guard. I would suggest a time of preparation to ready ourselves and our adherents for a larger strike. If we wished, we could always thin the herd should opportunities appear in the meantime."

The gnome shook his head. "No. We have momentum now and mustn't lose it. More successes will inspire more followers, increasing our numbers and building our influence on Earth."

Iressa stepped seamlessly into the gap as he paused. "We need not choose one or the other. We plan for a large act and hint about it to our minions, providing enough information to keep them hooked without going into detail. This addresses Ushev's concern." She raised a graceful palm to show off her long fingers adorned with rings and silence any potential detractors as she continued her speech. Her black nails glinted dangerously. "Then we distract the human authorities with smaller attacks in all the cities where our enemy is located. We use those assaults to occupy our foes, while we gather material and power. Then, it will all coalesce into a single mammoth strike where they least expect it."

Dreven made a show of considering her words. He had already decided to back her play and enjoyed the experience of hearing his own plans spoken in her voice. While he had believed all along that bigger was better, he'd allowed the group to try its more conservative approach. Success or failure in those efforts suited his needs, regardless. New developments required different plans, though. "I agree with Iressa. The time for bold action is now, but we can work both in the shadows and in the sunlight."

Jarkko growled. "We have to deal forcefully with these meddling humans. What we've done is clearly not enough. Stopping supplies is all well and good, but it does not send the message that they should fear us. They must learn that they are dealing with powers beyond their ability to control or even comprehend."

"I agree with the need to act against them directly," Pesharn said. "Several of my people have either died by their hands or now rot in captivity. We have underestimated this force time and again. They deserve respect as worthy adversaries, and they have earned our best efforts to destroy them before they can interfere again."

Ushev shook his head. "I disagree with placing so much of our focus on this new group of humans. Don't forget the other authorities. It would be foolish to disregard the Paranormal Defense group. There are others to consider as well. Fortunately, attacking any of them will be both easy and a good show for our followers."

Iressa's voice was disarmingly friendly. "We can and shall cause trouble for all of them, friend Ushev. But we must recognize those who interfered with the attack on the prison as our primary concern. They set themselves against us in a way the others have not, first in their capital city, and now in the one above the Kemana Stonehaven." She hissed the last word as if she were personally offended by the underground settlement.

Dreven nodded. "We will apply pressure against this group in every possible way. The politicians we own are already making plans to that end, and once we identify their new supply channels, they will be blocked as well."

Jarkko spread his burly arms wide. "And in the meantime, shall we simply wait? As Ushev has mentioned, we risk losing our momentum." Murmurs of agreement mingled with nods of approval traversed the circle in order until the floor was Dreven's again.

"In fact, there is a great opportunity at hand, a chance to make a statement as impressive as the one at the prison." Anger and suspicion greeted his contribution. He raised his hands placatingly. "Yes, this is new information, but I only learned of it recently and believed it could wait until this meeting." He gestured, and the projection of a suit of armor appeared over his closed fist. The image was slightly translucent as it rotated, and the pieces shifted from obsidian to scarlet and back again.

"Rhazdon's Defense," Pesharn whispered. The others' eyes widened at her identification of the item.

The wizard nodded. "Yes. As usual, the humans do not

know what they possess. This was unearthed at one of their archeological digs, and it is currently in transport. They are aware that it is powerful, and they are treating it with great care. There are three possibilities under discussion to deliver it to its destination in a mountain facility in Colorado. We will rely on our politicians to discover which is selected and strike to secure it for ourselves."

The dwarf barked a harsh laugh. "I'll look very good in that armor."

Pesharn growled, and Ushev laughed. Issera stared at Dreven with lustful promise on her face. He glanced away hurriedly.

*Sadly, none of us shall claim that prize, but that's not information you need at the present moment.*

"We can determine its use once we capture it. Doing so will require significant resources." The others nodded their heads in silent acknowledgment of their responsibility to provide said resources, namely in the form of forces to confront the humans. He dropped the protective shield to end the discussion.

The leaders disbanded without further comment. Issera departed with an exaggerated sashay that caused her dress to rustle across the ground. Jarkko clanked in counterpoint to Pesharn's heavy steps. Ushev was as silent as ever when he departed through his portal, and Dreven was finally left alone in the courtyard.

He paused for a moment to let his mind settle, then summoned his own portal and stepped through to his problematic underling's receiving room. Nehlan scampered in moments after his entry and bowed. "Welcome, Master. The table is being set. Please, come this way."

He gestured and fled the area. The elf's experience with the tentacles had fractured something in his spirit, which gave him the air of one desperate to satisfy and terrified of the consequences should he fail. Dreven was mostly convinced it was a true reflection but remained open to the possibility that his subordinate was somehow attempting to be clever.

*If he is, his efforts will fail as always.*

He entered the dining room, took the appointed seat, and cast a quick spell to block the entrance behind him. It was an insult to his host and recognition that trust between them was not what it should be due to his failures. He ate without fear, having long since secured his own antidote to the poisons Nehlan used. His subordinate sat and nibbled joylessly at his food as he waited for Dreven to pierce the silence.

*Definitely broken. Perhaps I left the tentacles on him for too long.*

The wizard swallowed and patted his lips with a heavy cloth napkin that matched the plates perfectly. "We will conduct operations against the humans who prevented you from kidnapping the ambassador and interfered in our attack on the prison. This is an opportunity for you to redeem some small part of your failure. Have you rebuilt your human forces?"

Nehlan didn't raise his eyes from his plate. "Y-yes, master. They are not of the same level of power, as none have been gifted with artifacts, but they are formidable."

Dreven nodded. "Very good. Send them out to gather information about our enemies and work with them to increase their skills. We won't underestimate this new opposition again. Your people will be called upon soon. And, perhaps, you personally as well."

The elf paled, and the wizard smiled.

*Repair yourself quickly, little minion, lest you find yourself discarded.*

# CHAPTER EIGHT

They entered the Capitol Building as tourists. Taggart took point and Cara and Diana trailed behind. The ARES leader seemed to possess a knack for disguise, first transforming himself into an unassuming older man, and then assisting them to change hairstyles and clothing choices to blend in better with the general public. Diana had been forced to trade her leather jacket for a Capitol varsity replacement, and Cara wore a decidedly boring sweater in an unattractive shade of beige.

It had been necessary to leave their guns at the SAC's office, but she had the non-metallic knives in her boots and the pepper spray that looked like mace attached to her key chain. Cara was never unarmed as long as she had at least two limbs remaining and would probably still be dangerous with only one. A certain Monty Python sketch played in Diana's mind as fake blood spurted from the black knight's shoulders. *Just a flesh wound.*

They separated from the tour shortly after it started

and entered an underground tunnel through an unmarked door. Taggart had explained they would meet in one of the several office buildings that served the Senate and House members. She lost track of their direction after a few minutes of twists and turns, but he eventually delivered them to a conference room. It was bigger than hers and featured a much larger oval table. Institutional tan walls were accented with a chair rail, a pair of whiteboards on opposite sides, and a prominent display at the front. They arrived to find the space empty, and Diana realized with a sad sigh that there wasn't a coffeemaker anywhere to be seen.

Taggart patted her shoulder sympathetically. "I don't know why anyone bothers to have meetings without coffee. They're asking for problems." He led them to seats along one side and sat between them. "Okay, so, this is an official briefing, such as it is. There won't be minutes or records, but in all other respects, this is where the big decisions are made. It's also where the council members attempt to manage us."

Cara laughed softly. "And how does that usually work out?"

The head of ARES DC grinned and brushed a hand through his crewcut. "Not as well as they'd prefer most of the time, I think." He leaned back in his chair. "Aaron Finley will be here. We like him and he's fairly sharp. Other than that, I'm not sure who else will attend. However, since they organized this gathering, it's likely we'll be graced with another senator or two."

"What do they want to talk about?" Diana asked.

He shrugged. "They haven't shared that information, but my money says it's about the Cube."

She pushed her momentary nervousness away. "What's your take, anyway?"

"Your team did excellent work. The council might complain about losing the building, but we didn't put any of the teams together with the expectation that they'd do bomb disposal. We already require that skill on all future rollouts, however, and plan to add them to existing locations."

Diana clasped one hand in the other to stop the incessant need to squeeze someone's neck for making trouble in her city. "Other than that?"

"Budget, warnings of things they've heard, more attempts to make us behave. There's no way to tell."

Further questioning was prevented when the door at the opposite end of the room banged open. Three people she recognized but hadn't met strode through in the midst of an animated discussion. They were soon followed by one man she definitely knew, Aaron Finley. She stood and shook hands across the table with each of the senators.

Finley made a round of introductions as they all found their places. He was positioned at the middle left, and the female senator was seated at the middle right. She was forty-something and radiated health and wealth from the top of her perfectly dyed black coif to the tips of her Ferragamo shoes. The hair fell in waves to her shoulders to frame a face that would have looked perfect on a movie star. Diana recalled coverage of her during the last election and had thought at the time that people would be crazy to vote for her. Her name was Janet Cyphret, the senior senator from South Carolina.

*Well, we're screwed now.*

Cyphret was vocally concerned with both the budget and the performance of multiple government agencies, and she had a reputation as a power-player. The woman looked at the men on either end of her side of the table and nodded grimly. Only one of them returned the gesture.

Naturally, she spoke first. Her sharp condescending tone made Diana want to grab a set of earplugs.

*Or a stun gun.*

"Your team's adventure in Pittsburgh was a dismal failure, Agent Sheen. What do you have to say for yourself?"

Taggart's light touch on her arm reminded her of the need for civility, regardless of the woman's provocation, and she reined in her initial impulse to respond with a level of snark appropriate to the question. "Ma'am, we successfully defended the prison from incursion. The enemy had not previously used explosives, so there was no reason to expect it. We responded to what confronted us in the moment, and no innocent lives were lost."

"No lives, but a multimillion-dollar building was very badly mangled."

"True, Senator. Unfortunately, it appears that someone who was read in on the project revealed the presence of the Cube and its location far ahead of time. That certainly wasn't within our purview."

The woman looked sufficiently mollified as she leaned back in her chair, although the twitch at the corners of her lips betrayed the smug smirk that lay behind the mask.

*Let's get into the ring, wench, and see what you're really made of.*

"SAC Taggart, do you feel that setting up additional locations is still viable, given the failures of the Pittsburgh office?"

Diana locked her muscles against the urge to stand and respond. Taggart's smooth drawl was calming, and she realized she only ever heard it when he tried to defuse a situation.

*He's a chameleon. I bet he was a Face at some point.*

"Failure is a strong word, Senator. The unit responded admirably and provided all the support Warden Murphy requested or required. Simply put, they did their jobs and did them well. The fact that we failed to predict the need for a bomb tech is a collective mistake that rests with everyone on every team—and with this council."

Cyphret smiled, and Diana immediately imagined her as a venomous snake that coiled and swayed, waiting for the perfect moment to strike. She returned her attention to Taggart and noted how expertly he wore his neutral expression. Cara was equally blank-faced. The senator opened her mouth to speak but was interrupted by the man on her right.

"Janet, quit badgering the agents. You know as well as I do that they did the best they could." Sam Somers was one of the longest-serving members of the Senate and represented Nebraska ably enough that he had never faced a serious primary challenge. He trounced the representatives of the other parties who tried for his seat regularly. The man was a noted centrist, and if there was a pragmatist party, he'd probably be the leading candidate to run it. "Agent Sheen, tell us, what could have been done better?"

*Finally, some sense. I'm glad at least one of these three has some.*

She smiled at the man. His snowy hair and carefully trimmed white mustache gave him an old-world charm that was only enhanced by the bolo tie he wore in place of the more common version.

"Senator Somers, I believe that we could have acted differently in three areas. First, we could have deployed armed drones to deal with the Kilomea before they arrived. Stun weapons would have been fine. We could have given them a warning and then eliminated them if they failed to heed it." That had been Cara's idea. Kayleigh was still dead-set against weaponized drones where public gatherings were involved.

Somers frowned. "Noted. We'll discuss that further amongst ourselves, as it clearly has far-reaching policy implications. Next?"

"The obvious lack of a demolitions expert. We are meeting with one whom we hope to add to the team tomorrow. That should go a long way toward—if you'll forgive the pun—defusing situations like we faced at the Cube."

The senator frowned again, and his fingers twitched in the meticulous habit of a regular note-taker. He scowled when he found no notepad with which to work and gestured for her to continue.

"Finally, it's time to take the fight to them, rather than being reactive to their movements. And in order to do that, we need to bring in better intelligence and require more latitude in our rules of engagement."

The sandy-haired man beside Cyphret broke his silence. Junior Senator Winston hailed from Louisiana, but his voice could have been from anywhere in the country.

*I wonder if he puts on a Creole accent when he's at home.*

The man leaned forward in a clearly aggressive stance as he glowered at her. "Perhaps new leadership is needed, given all these problems."

Taggart shrugged casually and continued in his neutral tone. "I serve at the council's pleasure, of course. But I believe that this is a bump in the road, not a true obstacle. Such action seems extreme given the course of events and the leadership demonstrated."

The thin man shrugged the shoulders of his perfectly tailored suit. If Diana had been obliged to describe him, she would have started with little rich boy. He wore a chunky watch, his haircut and clean shave were perfect, and an aristocratic air hung about him. If his face weren't so long, he would have been quite handsome, but as it was, he bordered on comical.

*He was probably made fun of all the time in school. Beaten up too, maybe. A girl can hope.*

"How did you address your supply shortages?" He changed subjects without warning. "I noticed that Sheen didn't mention them, so the issue must be resolved."

Taggart frowned and shook his head in disbelief at the question. "We have a technological line into their interception operations. I can't say more than that. It's a matter of operational security."

"Perhaps we should replace you with someone more

willing to share information with their superiors." Tomassi's glare was pure condescension.

"Do whatever you feel you must, Senator. I won't put my people in danger to provide you a level of detail that you don't actually need."

The man bristled and was about to reply when Somers interrupted. "Let's all stop being petty, please. Winston, any other questions for the agents?"

Tomassi nodded as he wrestled with the sneer that tried to manifest itself on his face. He finally mastered it, although it took a few seconds to do so. "Agent Sheen, how do you plan to address the apparent threat in your city?"

"I will find it and eradicate it, Senator."

"And do you have plans on how to do so?"

"Yes, sir. We have feelers out for any potential opportunities for them. Plus, we have surveillance on people we think are connected to the group. They appear to be low-level, but they might lead to someone bigger."

"How low?"

Her eyes widened at his continued demands for operational information.

*Maybe he simply wants to feel like a spy or something.*

"Street soldiers, mainly. We'll see where they go and who they talk to and work our way up the ladder."

Cyphret's smile was as oily as her hair. "We can't afford any more failures from your organization. Get your shit together, or changes in leadership will be made. At all levels." She stood and signaled the end of the meeting with a frosty farewell of, "Agents," before she turned and stalked from the room. Somers and Tomassi followed. The door hadn't even closed when their arguments began, faintly muffled until they faded completely.

Finley shook his head once the others had departed. "They're something, aren't they? You should see when the full Council gets together. It's like a nightmare of subtle and not so subtle back and front-stabbing."

Taggart's voice held several notes of concern. "What's the deal, Aaron?"

The senator spread his hands. "Other than the usual politics and power-mongering? Not positive. But both Cyphret and Tomassi are pushing on almost everything ARES-related lately—criticizing, seeking information, whispering to each other during meetings. I'm not fundamentally a paranoid person, but if I were you, I'd keep one eye fixed over my shoulder at all times."

Cara broke her silence. "The rest of the council can't rein them in?"

Finley swiveled his chair to face her directly. "No. This group tends to attract people canny enough to allow their enemies way out on a limb before they deal with them. Once they're there, though, it's a sharp chop and a long drop."

Diana sighed. "So they won't intervene until it's time to get rid of them."

"Exactly. It would ruin the drama of the moment, which can't be allowed."

"Let me guess, you're not a fan."

Both Finley and Taggart laughed before her boss spoke. "None of us are, but this is the hand we're dealt. Generally, they stay out of our way and are content to cause trouble for one another. That's probably the best outcome we can hope for."

Cara sighed. "You know, I'm more convinced than ever that we need armed drones. I've very recently met some people who would benefit from a good stun on a daily basis."

They all laughed, but Diana couldn't shake the feeling that something weird was going on with the council.

*Next time, I should bring Sloan with me. Maybe he'll have a sense of what they're up to.*

# CHAPTER NINE

Diana had never been to a Washington Nationals game before, despite being a fan of watching baseball at the ballpark. Her Dad had taken her to Rockies games when she was younger, and she and Bryant had already agreed to see the Pirates play sometime over the summer. He'd said the team wasn't awesome but the stadium was.

The three women wandered the upper deck, looking for the right concession stand. Lisa wore blue denim shorts and a white team jersey unbuttoned into a notably plunging V-neck.

*I guess there are worse places to find dates.*

Cara wore a jersey, too. This one was dark blue with a white tank underneath, and her jean shorts were a full inch longer than Lisa's. Both wore flip-flops like it was the middle of summer.

Diana had chosen her mostly normal look of black jeans, boots, and tank top. She'd hoped it would be warmer once they got out into the April sun. They reached the place they had searched for—a craft beer stand—and then found hot dogs with a variety of toppings to share and a couple of soft pretzels.

They carried the provisions down to their seats directly beside first base. Diana and Cara had argued about whether the baseline or behind home plate was superior, and Lisa had finally decided for them. Diana was glad to see her long-time friend thought the same way she did on the matter.

The other woman had groused about it in the car and finished with a, "Better watch that you don't take a baseball to the face, Lisa. It would wreck your beautiful looks. Diana...well, it would hurt."

Diana flipped her off from the passenger seat and changed the subject. It was true, she was the third-best looking in the group, but that was fine. Beautiful was not a prerequisite for awesome.

Lisa sat between them to keep the peace. Her black hair and flat eyes conjured the image of a female Confucius. "So, tell me about life up north."

Diana shrugged and finished chewing the too-large bite of soft pretzel she'd taken before she chased it with a solid drink of the cold beer.

*Delicious.*

"There is so much cool stuff going on, really. I learn about magic with a sadistic dark elf, get shot at regularly, and face constant insubordination from those I work with, especially the snarkiest lab tech ever known to humanity. Good times."

They laughed, and Cara added, "Plus, the always-present chance of an extra leg workout from being summoned to the kemana. And you forgot to mention the bounty hunts."

Diana groaned. "I'm trying to forget the bounty hunts. I'm not a stun-gun kind of girl."

Lisa looked from one to the other. "You're aware that you've only talked about work, right? Do you have a life at all?"

The ex-Marshall beat her to the answer. "Nope. All work, all the time."

"Work and Rath." Diana grinned. "Because, you know..." They all finished together. "Must train." The three broke into familiar peals of laughter and peace was restored.

"Well, I guess I'll start with the job, then," Lisa said. "It's not as awesome as it could be. The workload is increasing and they're not adding associates, so there's a ton of temps. That's brutal for morale. I think something is up and the partners aren't telling us what it is. So, in my spare time, I polish my resume."

"Just don't fall behind on your rent," Diana said wickedly.

Her friend laughed. "Witch."

"Wench."

They paused as the game began and the loudspeaker drowned out their conversation.

When play was underway, Lisa continued "The MMA stuff is going really well. I did briefly go out with one of the guys, though."

Diana wagged a chiding finger at her. "First rule. Don't date in the dojo. I warned you."

She sighed. "Screw your rules, Sheen. It was only a couple of dates, anyhow. We discovered we weren't compatible."

"Why not?" Cara asked.

"It turns out that despite my presence in class with him, he believes women belong in the home, barefoot and cleaning."

"Oh, hell no."

"Right?" Lisa laughed. "Anyway, I promised not to share that information as long as he left me alone. No issues so far."

Diana spread her arms wide and put one in Lisa's face. "And so the great wisdom of your best friend is confirmed, making her entirely superior to you in every—ow!" She clutched at the spot where Lisa had backhanded her in the solar plexus.

The blonde smiled beatifically as she asked, "No dates for you all?"

She shrugged. "I have no time. It's difficult being the boss, but someone has to do it."

Cara agreed. "Yep. Relationships take more effort than I have to spare. There'll be plenty of opportunity for that later. For now, there's always a date available a click or a swipe away."

Diana leaned over to look at her subordinate. "Well, aren't you the free spirit, romantically—and I use that term loosely—speaking?"

"Gotta live while you can, right? On any day, a job could go wrong and bang! Game over."

Lisa looked at her with a mock frown. "Quit being a downer. And when will 'later' come?"

She shrugged. "When taking care of trouble gets boring. So far, it's not. And besides, I'm not ready to be a single mom like Diana over there."

They all laughed. The stadium celebrated a home run by the home team, and they rose to join the crowd as they cheered. Once they returned to their seats, Diana retorted. "Rath is easy. Real single moms have it way harder than I do. I'd never be strong enough for that gig. I'll stick with dealing with magical threats any day of the week, thank you very much."

Lisa grinned. "How is the little monster?"

"He's good, although it seems like he lacks focus. For a while, it was all about training with Max, but they're a really great team now so there's not a lot of that left to do. He also has a sense of the neighborhood already, so he doesn't have a purpose to keep him motivated."

Cara leaned forward to be seen across Lisa. "Maybe you should give him one. At either of his smaller sizes, he'd make a good spy. He'd be able to get into unexpected places, that sort of thing."

Diana frowned. "A troll is obvious, though. Still, it might work. I worry about him out in the field, but the truth is that he seems rather self-sufficient."

The ex-Marshall scoffed. "He's totally carrying you, boss. We all know it. You can quit pretending."

"We'll figure something out. Also, you're an insubordinate jerk, and the next time we have a training run, I'll shoot you in the back."

Cara laughed, and Lisa said, "I have the solution. If I do lose my job, we can all move in together and it'll be like

Charlie's Angels. We'll be the Angels, and Rath can be Charlie."

The celebration of another home run drowned Diana's reply, but the solar plexus slap she delivered to reward Lisa for her earlier blow conveyed the message effectively.

*Rath would be way too into that.*

## CHAPTER TEN

The rental sedan was off-the-rack, unlike those they used at ARES. Its engine struggled and made the agent long for her Fastback. *Next time we drive to DC, to hell with this nonsense.* She took the turn onto the entry drive of Fort AP Hill and pulled into the lot outside HQ.

Cara was the first one out of the car and was clearly excited to be back on familiar territory. "You gotta love the military. Some things never change. I was here for specialized arms training at the same time as a Marine unit. We had some good competitions."

Diana nodded absently in response and looked at the building, a well-maintained structure set on large flat land with a row of hopeful trees on each side of the walk that led to the main entrance. Cara had described it as the largest construction on the base, which made it somewhat underwhelming when viewed in person. They stepped into the lobby and stopped before an Army corporal at a security desk. He verified their IDs and appointment and summoned a private to lead them along the left of the two wings that stretched toward the rear of the building.

Diana had expected an office or a conference room and was surprised when they entered a large classroom. Giant whiteboards hung on three walls, with student desks set in the middle.

Cara yelled, "Scully!" and a red-headed woman in camouflage fatigues turned with a grin.

Her voice was higher than Diana would have guessed but had a cheerful lilt. "Chicory, how the hell are you?" They bumped chests, then switched to a solid hug.

Cara waved her boss over. "Diana Sheen, this is Captain Dana Smithton, US Army Third Infantry. Dana, Diana is with me at the FBI." They had agreed to hide ARES under the auspices of the FBI with anyone not already read into the organization.

She nodded a greeting. "I get Scully. But why Chicory?" Cara looked at the floor and shook her head. The other woman laughed. She had a few freckles that went perfectly with her crimson mane, tamed into a professional bun, and was muscular and solid, taller than her—of course—and bigger overall than either of them. She'd be a formidable opponent on the mat.

Smithton grinned. "It's because of her last name. Binot is a lot like beignet, and we had a clerk who was from New Orleans, where they usually put chicory in their coffee. It was as good a nickname as any. Although some people had the wrong impression of 'chic' and had to be set straight."

Cara nodded at the other officer. "It has too many syllables for a callsign, though." She gestured at the whiteboard the woman had been writing on. "What are you teaching?"

Smithton shrugged. "The basics. Ballistics in general, characteristics of different rounds."

Diana examined the boards. The one at the front of the room held a drawing of a human figure. She pointed at it. "Do they learn something other than center mass these days?"

The captain shook her head. "No. That's for quick and dirty first aid for wounds received, assuming a medic isn't instantly at hand."

The third board was covered with the data they had come to see. Intricate diagrams of various explosives had been painstakingly drawn for the class to take notes. The dark hair and thick eyebrows of the man in front of the work provided a vague clue that he might be their man. That, his civilian outfit, and the fact he held a dry erase marker in his hand. An array of small scars that peppered one side of his face confirmed it. Diana excused herself and crossed to him. "Anik Khan?"

He grinned. "In the flesh. You must be Agent Sheen. I was just finishing up some prep for later. In case you couldn't tell, I teach these army youngsters how not to blow themselves up."

She extended a hand and he shook it with a confident grip."Thanks for making the time to talk to us. My second-in-command will come when she's done reliving the past over there."

Khan laughed deeply, throatily, and most importantly, warmly. Surprisingly enough, the man didn't have an accent. "Once Army, always Army."

A few minutes later, Cara joined them and introduced herself.

Anik set his marker down and looked at his watch. "I have an appointment with more advanced demolitions folks. Would you like to come along? We'll have time to chat after." Diana nodded, and they followed him out of the building. The ex-Marshall bumped her arm and gestured at the man's waist. She clearly admired the way his tight tactical pants fit.

Diana rolled her eyes as her friend chuckled and mouthed, "Gotta live."

He led them to an open-topped Jeep, and she claimed shotgun position. The teacher drove rapidly along the winding roads. Fortunately, there was no other traffic to be concerned about. A dense forest blurred past on their right. Cara explained how the base often used it for practical exercises and examinations. Khan pointed out the barracks, the mess hall, and other points of interest. After a few minutes, he steered the vehicle onto the grass behind a large roofless structure that reminded Diana of the gauntlet in DC.

The women followed him to a platform where he gestured them toward a table filled with gear. They selected helmets, glasses, and ear protectors as he waved the five soldiers lounging nearby into a circle with him at the center.

"All right, people. We have an OPFOR holed up inside and need to blow the obstacles. Each person will have a turn at a door. They're locked and blocked differently, so you'll have to evaluate the situation beforehand. I'll have the last set of gear in case one of you screws up." He grinned at them. "One mistake or less, we win, and you get a couple of hours of rest before lunch. Two mistakes or more, and you'll run a few miles as penance." A collective groan escaped the recruits' lips. "So, don't screw it up."

They geared up with laser tag gear and demolition packs, plus helmets, glasses, ear protectors, and Kevlar vests, and stood in a line. Khan gave the go signal, and the first soldier crouched before the door. He peered through the gaps and decided the best move was to attack the hinges. The instructor nodded in approval of the choice. He set small blocks of explosives at the top and bottom and attached the trigger, which had a battery built in for power. At another nod from Khan, he squeezed. The barrier blew inward and careened into the mannequin that waited inside, positioned to shoot at those coming through.

Khan signaled for them to advance. Diana and Cara trailed the group and watched as the soldiers used various placements to deal with different doors under the man's vigilant eye. The last was the most entertaining, as it was blocked with furniture. The team placed shaped charges all over it to blast through with a satisfying thump. When they finished, the instructor led them through a debrief and provided suggestions and refinements to each member. He gave them all pats on the shoulder or high-fives and sent them on their way.

The man grinned as he returned to the equipment table with his guests to dump their gear. "I love the smell of smoke and charred wood in the morning." They laughed, and he led them back to the Jeep. This time, Diana took the rear, and he steered the vehicle to the small canteen that served the officers and experts at the base. They received a meal of burgers and fries with a dose of strong coffee and sat to chat in the mostly empty space. Anik had wisely chosen the corner farthest from the few others who took advantage of an early lunch.

He caught Cara staring and turned the pockmarked side of his face to them with a grin. "Admiring my good looks, eh?" She blushed, and he waved her embarrassment aside. "It's not something I worry about. Honestly, it's not much worse than a wicked case of acne would have left behind, and it's definitely a better story."

The woman managed a sheepish smile. "So, tell us."

"All right. So, I was deployed in Afghanistan way back when. We were on a night raid into a bunker that was hidden under the floor of a house. I worked on setting the charges and had the positioned explosive on the corners and midpoints of each side, all wired to a single trigger that sat on the center. It was a little overkill, but we knew there was a metal door beneath the wooden one, so we needed to blast it hard." He shook his head. "Right after I set the last wire in place, but before I could get clear, they sprung an ambush, knocked our sentry back, and opened fire into the room. A couple of people caught bullets, but I managed not to. Simply good fortune, really."

He shrugged. "My luck ran out when a bullet hit the trigger perfectly and detonated the charges. I was already moving away, but the wooden door disintegrated, and splinters exploded everywhere. If I hadn't worn my glasses, they would have blinded me on that side. Fortunately, all they did was knock my supernatural good looks to standard human levels, luckily for the ladies."

Both women choked as they laughed around their food or drink, and he leaned back with a satisfied grin.

Diana wiped the tears from her eyes. "How'd you get

from there to here?"

"State police needed an expert. I needed a change of pace after too many days in the field. It's worked out well. But, as you can see, I keep my hand in."

"So, why the interest in changing again?"

He took his time over another bite of burger. "My goal in life is basically to cause trouble and blow stuff up. I spend most of my time now making things not blow up which, while exciting in its own way, isn't as much fun as making them go boom. Plus, I've done this for a while. This feels like a good moment to shake up the status quo."

She pushed her tray aside and leaned forward. "So, what questions do you have for us?"

"Tony covered most of the basics on the phone. But he wasn't clear on why me or why now, so that's what I want to know."

Her grin was deliberately casual. "You might have heard about an office building exploding in Pittsburgh?"

He laughed. "It'd be hard to miss that story."

"Well, that was my group. it would have been good to have someone who could have done something about the explosives. But, more than that, we face a higher level of opposition than we expected. Everyone on the team needs to be able to fight, so military or FBI are good sources. I'm confident there will be many opportunities to blow things up."

Cara added, "Plus, you'll get to collaborate with our tech on new and exciting ways to do it." She paused, her expression teasing. "Blow things up, I mean."

Her boss slapped her lightly on the arm. "Behave, or Kayleigh will have her revenge."

Anik's eyes widened. "Dornan? Kayleigh Dornan?" She nodded. "She did some work with the State Police a while back. It seems she had to put a person or two in their places, though, at the start."

Cara laughed. "She's fierce, no question. And easily underestimated."

"So, where do we go from here? It sounds like a sweet gig." He grinned.

Diana returned the smile. "It is a sweet gig, or at least we all think so. Standard procedure is that first, we talk about you behind your back." He laughed. "Then, we do a short probationary period to make sure we're a good fit for each other. We run down a few bounties, that sort of thing. Do you have any vacation time, or can you take leave for a while?"

"Either or both." He nodded.

"Cool. If we decide you're worthy of joining us for a tryout, someone will be in touch in the next few days." She softened the statement with a smile. "Then you can come up, we'll stash you in a hotel, and away we go."

They rose as one and traded handshakes. He gave them a smug grin. "Well, then, I'll see you soon." He dropped the smugness and laughed as he spread his arms wide. "After all, who could resist this?"

On the way to the airport, the women agreed on three things. First, that Anik was hard to resist when he turned on the charm. Second, that he would be a great addition to the team. And finally, that maybe a good-looking demolition man would be the thing to keep Kayleigh in town for a while longer if only to disabuse him of the notion that he was as appealing as he thought.

# CHAPTER ELEVEN

Diana guided the ARES SUV through the city streets on the north side of town. She and Cara were both worn out from the trip from Virginia via Reagan International in DC, but the opportunity she'd waited for had come. The warden of the Cube had agreed to let them interview the enemy they'd extracted from the exploding office building.

Arrival at the site was very different than before that particular adventure. The location of the former structure was now empty soil, quickly cleared by the army at the request of ARES' oversight council. A blockhouse stood where the lobby had once been and extended over part of the leveled area beside it. After the fact, Warden Murphy had revealed that the building had been one more decoy. The facility's elevators traveled sideways as well as down and moved away from the visible portion.

*Secrets hiding other secrets, all the way to the bottom.*

A twelve-foot fence with razor wire surrounded the boundary of the facility, and a pair of armed guards stood at the front of it. Diana pulled up and pressed her palm to the tablet the first man extended, and his partner opened the gate when the two were cleared. She eased to a stop beside the blockhouse and parked between two black sedans with extra antennas.

They hurried to the entrance and she beat Cara to the door by a step and tugged it open. The lobby was mostly the same, except for the additional armed guard on either side of the new counter. It wasn't as heavy as the old desk, which she'd last seen in the hands of a Kilomea who used it as a shield. An invader wouldn't be able to repeat the stunt a second time and escape unscathed.

They navigated the security procedure and reached the elevator lobby, then descended to the first underground level. Warden Murphy waited to greet them with a smile on her thin face and led them into the viewing portion of interview room three. The dark space was filled with a row of chairs that faced the one-way mirror to offer a perfect view of the interrogation area beyond. The heavy plastic chair was empty, which provided a clear view of the articulated sections that could be manipulated to make an occupant either more secure or deliberately uncomfortable. Metal circles had been incorporated throughout the design to deliver shocks as necessary.

Murphy gestured them to two chairs and took the one at the end of the row for herself. "So, has everyone recovered from our little adventure?"

Cara laughed. "That was the most fun I've had in months."

Diana shook her head. "We're all good. How did your defenses work out?"

The warden ran her hands through her shortish brown hair. "Adequately. They couldn't break in, as predicted. Another pack of Kilomea tried a sneak attack from the opposite side after yours started trouble in the office building." She grimaced. "Anyway, we were able to drive them away with drones."

"Stun guns?" Cara asked.

"At first. But they didn't work very well, so we had to bring out the real weapons. By that time, the crowd had been pushed back enough that we could do it safely. We swung them so any misses would hit the buildings."

Diana straightened abruptly in her chair. "Did you have any fallout?"

Murphy shook her head. "No. If anyone noticed, they haven't complained. It's not something I did lightly and not something I'd like to do again. But desperate times..."

*Call for desperate measures. I know very well, actually.*

"Did you round up any of them afterward?"

"A couple more Kilomea to join your friend. None are as annoying as he is, though."

"Is Crisnan behaving himself?"

"More or less. He's asked about news from outside, according to the guards who watch the common area. That's not unusual, but his questions seem to be focused on the Remembrance. If it weren't so unlikely, I'd say he thinks a rescue is coming."

Cara laughed. "Not in this place. It would take a bunker-buster simply to get inside."

The woman smiled. "We like to think so, anyway."

Diana thought about the Kilomea who'd dented her car

and decided she was game for a third round with him if such an opportunity ever came up.

*Especially now that I have my magic mojo rising.*

"What about the chucklehead we dropped off?"

The warden barked a laugh. "It's funny. When they designed the place, having non-magicals as prisoners wasn't actually considered. I guess they were so focused on the one thing that they forgot the other. Marcus is easy since he's only human, but we'll keep him out of the general population. That's also easy since he's been in the infirmary from the day of his arrival." She looked at her watch. "Perfect timing."

The door to the interrogation chamber opened and two burly guards escorted the man Cara had defeated in the office building into the room. He displayed a smug smile while they strapped him into the chair. His collar-length hair was disheveled and matted, and his face was strangely flat. It gave him character, and she wouldn't find him unattractive under normal circumstances, although he was fairly skinny. It wasn't until they were securing his right arm that Diana noticed they couldn't do the same with the left because it was no longer there. The limb ended at the shoulder, where a bulge in his baggy orange jumpsuit suggested bandaging beneath.

"What happened to his arm?"

Murphy shrugged. "By the time the raid was over, it was too far gone to save. We brought in the best team of surgeons from the nearest hospital, but they couldn't do anything except remove the damaged parts. It was simply too late, even for a healing potion. The fight started it, and the explosion finished it, they said."

Diana looked at Cara, whose expression of contempt for the man hadn't changed.

*Good. He chose his path. It's not our fault it was a bad decision. But to make sure...*

"Cara, are you up for this?"

Her second-in-command grinned and spoke without a hint of hesitation. "Completely. Let's do it."

Warden Murphy took them to the door and let them into the cell. The prisoner didn't react when Diana stepped in but growled at the sight of the other agent. She gestured for Cara to take the lead since she was already under the man's skin and leaned her back against the mirrored wall.

The ex-Marshall walked slowly toward him "Hey, scumbag. How's prison? I hope you're not in too much pain." She shook her head in mock commiseration. "Too bad about the arm. I suppose you should have paid more for your tiny, inadequate backup gun."

He snarled contempt. "Bitch. Let me out of this chair and I'll teach you what suffering really is."

She laughed. "Even being in the same room with you is more than enough suffering for me, thanks. Although it is fun to see you all locked down like that."

He relaxed and a smile crept onto his face as his eyelids slid halfway closed. "We'll have the chance to dance again. You have no idea what you're up against. No idea at all."

"Illuminate me, big boy." She leaned on the arms of the chair and put her face near his.

He tried to headbutt her, but she yanked her face away in plenty of time. She had clearly anticipated that reaction.

The prisoner grinned. "I knew you were playing me,

but I had to try anyway. It's always possible you could be as dumb as you look."

She placed a hand over her heart. "You wound me."

He bared his teeth. "That's only the start of what I'd like to do to you."

"I notice that you're avoiding the question. The whole, 'you don't know what you're up against thing' is merely talk like the rest of you, I guess? I'm sure you tell everyone you're a good fighter when you're really a punk."

The prisoner leaned forward as far as the restraints would allow and laughed. "I'm not an idiot. You can't play me, bitch. But I'll give you this for free—something big is coming, and you've put yourself directly on the tracks in front of it. When it runs you over, I'll be there to watch it happen."

Cara turned to Diana. "How about we store him in general population for a while? Let's see if that changes his attitude. Wounded prey like him won't stand much of a chance against the Kilomea hunting instinct."

He laughed again. "Do it. I'll be leading them in a day, and they'll break me out in a week. I'm a survivor, lady. This"—he waved his hand in a circle as large as the restraints allowed—"is only a vacation for me."

The ex-Marshall stepped in front of him again, a hair's breadth out of reach, and patted him on the top of the head. "You keep thinking that, little guy. I'll be back next week, and the week after, and the week after that. Eventually, you'll realize that what you call a 'vacation' is really the rest of your life. I'm sure you'll get bored, and then angry, and then hopeless. And I'll be here, watching, every step of the way."

"Until next time, then, skank."

She stepped back with a nod. "Until next time, *survivor.*" Diana was impressed at the amount of condescension that Cara was able to pack into one word. The man in the chair flinched and a crinkling at the corner of his eye showed that the jibe had found its mark.

The door unlocked as they approached, and Warden Murphy awaited them in the hallway. Once the locks thumped closed again, she grinned at the interrogator. "Well done. I was surprised you didn't go for a little shock action."

Cara shook her head. "I'll have plenty of opportunity for fun and games with that one, it seems. Has he been like this since he got here?"

"No. He's been very quiet. If I had to draw a conclusion, I'd say he's biding his time, waiting for the rescue he also appears to think is coming."

Diana frowned. "That's not a good sign, especially when Cresnan has the same stupid idea. Would you be willing to allow us to bring in an empath to be a part of the next interrogation?"

Murphy nodded. "Absolutely. Anything you need."

She sent a text to Bryant with the request and received an immediate affirmative in reply. "Okay, we'll set it up. In the meantime, do you think the Cube is in danger?"

The warden shrugged. "We're always in danger, I'm sure, but not much more than before. We have our fence, we have our drones, and we're well protected underground."

Cara tapped her chin with a finger. "And yet, something doesn't feel quite right about all of this, does it?"

*Yeah. Exactly.*

Diana took her first steps toward the elevator lobby and assumed the others would follow. "We won't figure it out hanging around here. It's time to hit the streets and see what we can find out—and to get Kayleigh working on some better surveillance patterns." She sighed. "I guess our vacation is over, too."

Cara laughed. "Every day is a vacation in this job, boss. Pass the sunscreen."

# CHAPTER TWELVE

Vincente paced restlessly in front of the large windows that overlooked the warehouse below. His stomach itched where the artifact had sunk into his skin as though it somehow judged him for the failure. Summoning a portal to the World in Between had been a move planned long in advance as a way to dispose of the enemy with a minimum of fuss. The damn woman was defeated, right up until the moment the bloody troll knocked his magical second-in-command into the rift.

He snarled at the unfairness of it all. He'd lost both his seconds in one misadventure, and it was a challenge to keep their people in line. The human half proved easier to manage. The promise of riches and chaos as they continued to pursue the goals of the Remembrance sufficed to hold their interest. Factions jostled for position, but no clear frontrunner had emerged. He had reassured them that they would retrieve Marcus from his imprisonment as soon as it could be arranged.

Sarah's followers were harder to distract and delay, so he had agreed to do something he absolutely did not want to do. Below, they prepared for the event and finalized the magical pattern on the cement floor of the space. He sighed, crossed to the safe, unlocked it, and withdrew his bracelet. He'd had the magic item for years. It was capable of generating an impenetrable shield for a short duration according to the research he'd undertaken after discovering it. Deciphering the activation phrase had taken far too much time and effort, but it had provided him with this one final backup. He hoped he wouldn't need it but honestly feared that he would.

The wizard checked to ensure that his two wands were in place inside the sleeves of his jacket, ready to slide into his hands at the appropriate flick of the wrist. The coat was black, and the button-up shirt beneath it and the accompanying tie were the same. Even his boots and trousers matched. If today was to be his last day, he would go out in style. His low heels clicked on the steel stairs as he descended slowly while he focused his will on the task ahead.

He stopped halfway down and ran a critical eye over the circles that had been carved into the now empty floor of the space. A wide ring formed the perimeter, filled with shining white-grey metal engraved with magical runes. Inside it lay a narrower ring of an orange-tan metal engraved with similar runes. A circle was defined by crystals set into the floor at the eight points of the compass in the center. As he watched, Sarah's followers stepped into position. Four stood in the area between the copper ring and the faceted gems, the most powerful witches and wizards of the group. The rest were positioned between the two metal rings, equally distributed around the circle.

Vincente finished his descent and strode to the center. They had used the crystals' defenses each of the previous four nights as they sent signals into the World in Between to draw Sarah to them. Tonight would call for the ring's full protection, as they would need to keep the portal open until he had retrieved her. It was the right thing to do for her, and it was also essential to maintain control over her followers. Loathe though he was to admit it, they comprised his power base, and he couldn't afford to lose them.

Still, if he could have opted out, he would have done so without any qualms.

*Well, without much hesitation, at least. There's an argument to be made that I owe her something for her loyalty. Maybe.*

He sighed, then rolled his neck and nodded at the people ahead of him.

Those in the silver ring raised their wands and channeled their power into a pair of shields. The outermost barrier would prevent any external magic from entering and disrupting the ceremony. The inner shield would hinder anything that made it out of the rift from escaping —provided, of course, that they were strong enough to sustain it. Those on the inside of the barriers with him would maintain the portal to the World In Between and deal with any creature from the void who broke free. That was the plan, at least.

At his next nod, the four nearest the gems focused their

wands and created a thin hole in reality that revealed the chaotic middle ground that lay between Earth and Oriceran. Faces flickered in front of the translucent rift, and a hint of the nightmarish landscape was visible behind them, hidden by the mist that filled the space. Already, the ominous sense of monsters waiting immediately beyond with waving tentacles permeated the air. It was entirely likely that they knew something was coming and that a means had also been prepared to keep them on their plane of existence. Anything that came through would encounter determined resistance.

Vincente swallowed his fear.

*I will not be denied. My glorious future awaits beyond this act.*

He cast the spell to finish the bridge to the other world. The translucence faded into a reality with most of the color washed out of it, rendered in grey and sickly crimson. His forces created barriers to each side, which allowed him to step through and narrow the angle the denizens of the hellscape could use to attack him. Formless beings screamed but he ignored them. Sound was nothing. Hideous creatures danced in the distance, promising torment and demonstrating their prowess, but he ignored them as well. Their threats were nothing. Only his purpose and the imminent perils to it mattered.

The expected and feared tentacles materialized and attacked from every vector as two monsters from nightmare appeared on either side. Sharp teeth and spines complemented the barbs on the whips that lashed at him. A calm spell and gesture protected him from their impact, and another drove them screeching away with a bright beam of light. The power scattered the less dire beasts that accompanied them.

He sensed Sarah before she was close enough to see. The monsters seemed attracted to her living presence the way a plant reached toward the sun. He knew she approached from the right and cast his own wall before him, calling for her followers to create a gap for her to use. His vision cleared in that direction as they obeyed and he saw her in the middle distance, running headlong toward them. Her garments were ripped and shredded, her hair wild and unkempt, and there was a decided limp in her left leg that doubtless caused her pain with every step of her lurching sprint.

Behind her ran hordes of the trapped, those whose deeds in the real world were so dire that they wound up here by one mechanism or another. They lived a half-life at best, as the place drained the vitality from them.

*If I had to choose this or Trevilsom, I'd choose the prison.*

A winged creature attacked from above, and he barely managed to raise his second wand to deflect it, as focused as he was on holding the enemy at bay until she arrived.

His foes on the ground took advantage of this moment of distraction and threw themselves into the gap between him and the woman he was there to rescue. He growled defiance, called upon the artifact within, and summoned his own shadow tentacles to eliminate the monsters that threatened her. The appendages seemed extraordinarily powerful, unlike the rest of his magic which pulled vital energy from him with each spell. They stretched and swayed and cleared the way for the fleeing witch before the enemies could complete their blockade.

In the next moment, she was through. Her momentum didn't stop and she continued to run, and Vincente threw himself after her. One of her followers had disobeyed instructions and entered behind him, doubtless seeking to distinguish himself to her with his bravery. It was a foolish sentiment. The man was captured by a swarm of tentacles and dragged beyond hope of assistance. Vincente had neither the time nor the inclination to intervene. He barely had the time slide through the rift himself after the foolish acolyte's supporting power drained from the spell that maintained the portal.

The aperture collapsed as he crossed the threshold. A severed tentacle flopped behind him until a mage in the inner ring vaporized it with a venomous incantation. Sarah crumpled on the floor, her face down, huddled inside herself. The air of menace that radiated from her dissuaded anyone who might have offered assistance from approaching.

Vincente pushed slowly to his feet and checked to make sure the portal had fully closed. He poked at the charred tentacle with a toe, then pointed at those around them and indicated they should depart. Some did so with alacrity. Others clearly resented the dismissal, but they all complied. Small sounds between whimpers and laughter emerged from beneath Sarah's dark hair. He was prepared to stand there for as long as she needed to regain herself and definitely was neither brave nor foolish enough to attempt to brace her before she was ready.

She finally shuffled first to her hands and knees, then stood with an awkward, stiff struggle. Her shoulders indicated her heavy breathing as she kept her back to her superior while she pieced her composure together. Finally, she straightened with an obvious effort and ran her fingers through the rat's nest of hair atop her head. She succeeded in pushing it out of her face, but it remained knotted and disheveled when she turned. Vincente steeled himself.

It was good that he had. Her skin was ashen as if her stay in that hellscape had scoured the color away. Three partially healed diagonal wounds covered each cheek and appeared to be the right size to have come from her own nails. Her eyes showed the greatest change, however. What had once been sarcastic mirth and zealous devotion had frozen into the harsh gaze of a survivor, filled with cruelty and rimmed by madness. She grinned and displayed several broken teeth. Her voice rasped accusingly. "You took your time, didn't you?"

He flinched at the sound but forced steel into his spine. "Recovery took time. Finding you took time. Drawing you took time. We worked as quickly as we could."

*Once it became obvious that you were still needed, anyway.*

Her grin widened, and he barely suppressed an involuntary shudder.

*Has she developed telepathy as well?*

Vincente actually stumbled over his words in his haste to continue. "I'm sorry for the loss of your follower." He gestured toward where the rift had been.

She rubbed her hands slowly down her arms and on to smooth what remained of her long dress. "No matter. He served his purpose, and in doing so, served my purpose. Now, I am free to bring Rhazdon's vision to life, to make the humans kneel or die." The way she licked her teeth so openly indicated exactly how much she desired the latter.

When she'd finished feasting on that thought, she turned her gaze on him. The cruelty and madness came to a sharpened focus as her stare bored into him. "You will secure a wand for me. And an artifact, as you promised."

*Shit. I'd hoped she'd forgotten about that.*

He nodded but didn't trust himself to speak. His feet shifted and his body swayed, then froze as the stare became a glare. She clearly didn't want to show any signs of weakness. He waited in silence as she finished primping herself. The various actions and movements proved awkward and somehow sensual. Then again, perhaps it was the danger that attracted him. He'd always made bad decisions about women in his personal life.

She noticed his study and smiled at him from under the hair that had slipped past her ear as she finished adjusting her clothes. "Perhaps, when the humans are brought to heel, there will be time for other…diversions."

Vincente wondered for a brief moment if it would be better for everyone concerned if she was no longer counted among the living. Sarah grinned and raised an eyebrow as if she again listened in on his thoughts. After a small shrug, she turned and stalked out of the front door of the warehouse without another word. Her destination was unknown, but she would be back. That much was certain.

He stared at where she'd been for a protracted time after she'd left. Two things were clear. First, he would need to keep his human followers far, far away from his magical lieutenant and her people lest they be killed out of hand. Second, the odds that he would survive a battle with her were even at best—and probably worse—which meant he needed to accede to her wishes as long as they didn't stop his progress toward his own goals.

He sighed and shook his head as he began his ascent to the office.

*I guess I'd better arrange that artifact for her.*

## CHAPTER THIRTEEN

Rath waited while the flood of students passed through the doorway and tapped Max to slip inside before it closed. The classroom was located in a different building a couple of streets away from the tower that held Professor Stanley's office. This structure was smaller, far less interesting, and would have been a good candidate for something to blow up in an action movie, given how out of date it looked.

The classroom itself was wonderful, with a huge display mounted on the front wall. Tables sat on risers that ascended to the back of the room. Charlotte had told him he might be most comfortable up there, so he directed Max to the stairs. They took position in the rear corner, with the troll perched on a nearby table while the Borzoi rested beneath it.

Students wandered in over the next ten minutes with drowsy expressions. Each chose their seating with some form of shared understanding of location that Rath wasn't privy to. The activity started off with tiny scatterings of one and two. Over time, more people entered to connect the separate groups until almost every seat was filled. Eventually, a man in an oversized hoodie took a seat at Rath's table.

"Hello, little dude," he greeted cheerfully, laid his head on the table, and started snoring a few seconds later.

Professor Charlotte Stanley swept into the room with a dramatic swirl of her blue skirt. She typed something into the computer at the front. Her cardigan matched the skirt with a white blouse and silver necklace under the sweater. The lights dimmed, and an image appeared on the screen portraying a painting of a magical battle. Her soft voice issued from the speakers mounted on the walls.

"This work commemorates the first of two seemingly final battles against Rhazdon and, at the time, her followers."

She zoomed in on a part of the image. "Here you can see members of the royal family commanding the armies opposing the rebels." Rath heard a distinct *click* and watched as the image blurred, then focused on a different position. "And here you can see Rhazdon's disciples. What's notable about them?"

A short silence threatened to become a long one before a small woman with dark hair in the front row raised her hand. Charlotte nodded at her. The student seemed to ask rather than to state her suggestion. "There are multiple different beings in that group."

The professor smiled at her. "Exactly, Theresa. Thank you." She turned to face the rest of the room. "Rhazdon shared a simple message—that power belonged in everyone's hands, not only in those who ruled by the good fortune of high birth. It resonated with many and crossed most of the traditional lines that foment unrest—species, gender, and all the other ways we tend to label ourselves."

She raised her arms toward her audience. "You've read about this already. You tell me. Who was in the right?"

A spirited discussion ensued among the students, moderated by well-timed comments from the professor. It wove through the many issues involved in the situation—power, class, race, gender, and more. The opinions seemed fragmented, each advocating for the particular piece of the puzzle that most resonated with them.

*Just like how it probably was back then,* Rath thought. *People seeing that which was closest to them and not necessarily the whole picture. Perfect pawns for those with broader vision.*

Eventually, the student next to him, who had woken up and paid an impressive amount of attention during the class, turned to him and spoke loudly enough for the room to hear. "Hey, little dude, what do you think? Was the royal family wrong to hang onto power the way they did?"

The troll shrugged as the class turned their collective gaze on him for the first time. Many were surprised by their unexpected guest. Charlotte smiled and stalked up the aisle to stand beside him. She held her clip microphone out on its cord so he could speak into it.

"Don't really know. Wasn't there. But with great power comes great responsibility. Maybe everyone forgot that."

There were murmurs of assent and some smirks mingled with applause for the reference. Charlotte smiled at him, and his relaxed companion held a hand out for a high five. The class moved quickly on to further discussion of the history around Rhazdon's group. Rath had other things to ponder.

*What responsibility does the Remembrance think it has? To who? Against who? Everyone?*

He was more a live-in-the-moment kind of troll than a far-thinking one, but the potential answers to those questions left him feeling decidedly uncomfortable.

After class ended, he and Max bounded out of the room and ran to the teahouse where they'd promised to meet Professor Stanley. They slid through the door as others departed, as usual, and had a table of their own by the time she arrived. She went to the counter first and finally joined them, bearing cups for each of her guests. Rath grew to his three-foot size in order to drink it. When the first bubble of tapioca burst in his mouth, he realized why Charlotte liked it so much and gave her a happy grin. "Is good."

She nodded and took a long sip of her own before she set a bowl of water down for Max. "It is. So, did you enjoy the class today?"

He shrugged. "Many people. Many ideas. Hard to come together."

Charlotte leaned back and sighed. "You can say that again, my friend. And if it's challenging in the classroom—where at least we all have the shared mission of learning—how much harder is it out in the world? Very, I would say." He nodded in agreement and she leaned forward again. "Are you aware of the motives behind the attack on the prison? There have been whispers that those responsible are new followers of Rhazdon."

He frowned, wondering how that information had been

revealed, then decided it didn't really matter. "Heard the same. Not sure how true. Could be stealing the name only."

The professor nodded. "That makes sense. Well, in any case, I hope they are dealt with before they can do more damage."

"Me too." Max made a soft chuff of agreement from his position at their feet. They talked of other things while they finished their tea, wandered to the sidewalk together, and said their goodbyes. Rath shrank and hopped on Max's collar, and they sauntered down the street. As he swung back to wave farewell a final time, Charlotte turned into an alley a block away. He frowned.

*That doesn't seem very smart.*

He tapped the dog to turn him. "Quiet, Max. Stealthy." The Borzoi padded ahead quickly and soundlessly and moved low to the ground. People on the sidewalk stared at the dog and the tiny troll as they slunk past, but Rath paid them little mind. He was worried about the professor. Max moved only far enough that they could look down the alley and they saw her turn into another across a small street. "Faster, Max," he urged. They raced after her and reached the next alley in time to watch what unfolded.

The narrow passage was barely wide enough for three people. Halfway down the shaded path, a pair of tough-looking individuals walked a menacing circle around Charlotte, who waited calmly between them. Both stood taller than her and wore dirty jeans and hooded sweat-shirts. One kept the hood up. The other was bald with several silver hoop earrings in each ear. His voice emerged in a condescending growl. "Give us the purse, lady. Don't make us hurt you."

The other echoed the order. His voice sounded higher and faster like Diana did when she'd had too much coffee. "Yeah, give us the purse."

She looked at her handbag, then at the would-be muggers. Her position was such that Rath could see the amused look on her face, which seemed totally inappropriate for the moment. "This purse? Right here?" She held the shoulder bag up. "Oh, no. I couldn't possibly. It has all my stuff in it. My students' papers, for one, and that's a big no-no. Privacy and whatnot. Certainly, you understand. How about I buy you both a coffee and we talk about changing the direction of your lives, instead? There's a shop around the corner."

The troll narrowed his eyes. It still sounded like the woman he knew, but different, somehow—stronger, more confident, and direct. The men didn't quite know how to react, it seemed, because they stood in silence for a long moment. Finally, the bald one punched a fist into his palm. "Right, a beating it is." He stepped forward and swung a looping hook at the professor's head, but she was no longer there.

Charlotte ducked and spun out of the way with more agility that Rath would have expected, and his respect for her grew at the sight.

*Professor Charlotte clearly trains.*

He was even more surprised when a wand appeared in her hand and she used it to retaliate with invisible bolts of force that hurled the thieves into the walls on either side. They slumped in a daze, now devoid of all trace of aggression. The woman smiled and tapped each one lightly on the skull with her wand and muttered a word. Both men fell still.

The entire conflict—if one wanted to call it that—took only seconds. She stood over her attackers, shook her head, and muttered irritably to herself. Rath only caught a few of the words, which included "stupid" and "bad choices." She knelt beside one and pointed her wand at the space where the wall met the concrete surface of the alley. Her lips moved briefly before she straightened and resumed her stroll. It didn't take long for her to exit onto the next street.

The troll dismounted and grew to his medium size as he approached the fallen men. A tiny part of him feared what he might find, but he discovered to his relief that they only slumbered. His attention was captured by a subtle glimmer, and he knelt to peer at the spot where her wand had been pointed. The reflection was a stylized outline of a lion's body with the beak and wings of a giant bird that glinted in silver when he shifted his head to the right angle. He shrugged, withdrew his small smartphone from the pouch attached to Max's collar, and took a picture of it. Then, he snapped images of the criminal's faces to add to the records at the base and stowed the device again.

He paused as he was about to shrink and jump back on the dog's back and considered whether he should call the police to pick them up but shook his head.

*No. Charlotte didn't, so I won't. I wonder what she's up to.*

Then, he grinned. The city needed people who were willing to do good, and it looked like Charlotte was part of the team, exactly like him, Max, Diana, and the others.

*Great responsibility. We are the law.*

# CHAPTER FOURTEEN

"I'm sorry we didn't get a bounty run or two in before you guys had to roll out on a real mission." Diana strapped her shin guards on and watched to be sure that Anik Khan and Sloan Woodham were familiar enough with the lockers to find their gear. Neither seemed to have any trouble. Their new Face had spent several days familiarizing himself with the facility, and even though the demolitions expert had only arrived the day before, he was used to working out of different locations and adapted with ease.

Kayleigh entered the room, walking slowly as she reviewed something in her AR glasses. Haptic sensors stuck like ornaments on her fingernails allowed her to manipulate the data through hand motions. "Okay, people, listen up. PD surveillance grid spotted a pack of Kilomea crossing the rooftops at the side of the strip district that caters to the gem trade. The early guess is they'll do a smash and grab at one or more of the dealers in the Desotte building." The structure was part of the city's past and stood only five stories high, but it was the historical location for the highest-end jewelry buyers and sellers in town. Many dealers still worked in the building and the surrounding area.

"There are eight of them, and I have a drone on the way, about a minute out. And before you ask, Cara and Tony, no, it's not armed." Both agents groaned loudly for effect and she scowled. "SWAT will create a perimeter after we arrive so as not to spoil the surprise."

Diana cut in. "We've requested they stay out of this and let us handle it, rather than going in together like we did at the museum. I think we should be able to divide and conquer. As far as gear goes, we don't want to blow the place up more than we have to, so stick to flashbangs, sonics, and pepper. They should all tick the Kilomea off as much as they do wizards and witches. We shouldn't need anti-magic bullets against them, but make sure you have at least one magazine for each weapon, plus your backup filled with the little buggers. You never know."

She crossed to where the stun rifles rested on the wall and pulled them down. After a brief examination, she handed them to her compatriots. "Half of us will go in the top, and the others will enter from the bottom. SWAT has a key or something to get you inside."

"You know, boss, what we really need is a mobile armory for situations like these. We could already be there by now," Cara said.

"I'm way ahead of you and have already kicked the idea up to Bryant. He kicked it right back with a hard no. So, eventually, we'll have to make it happen on our own." The members of her team who knew the regional SAC laughed.

The newest recruits hadn't met him yet, so they didn't quite get the joke. "Rath, Sloan, and I are upstairs. Everyone else will enter through the front door."

They stood while they finished gearing up and paired off for a final equipment check. Kayleigh waved her hand in the air a few times. "Okay, the drone's in place high enough that they can't hit it. I'd rather not have a repeat of the incident at the Cube, thank you very much."

"Are you still sore over that knife throw? Come on. You have to admit that was cool," Cara teased.

"And I suppose you're willing to buy me a new drone out of your paycheck, then?" the tech asked icily.

She merely winced in response.

"I'm glad we understand each other." She cleared her throat. "Back to business. I've confirmed entry. The raiding party looks like a group of eight and they've chosen the roof."

Diana shook her head. "Eight of them, six of us. It hardly seems fair."

"For them." Cara smirked and gave Tony a high five.

Rath grinned. "Never tell me the odds."

Cara shot Diana a look and mouthed, "Yes, *Star Wars* marathon."

The other woman rolled her eyes. Out loud, Diana said, "Go check." Six responses echoed. Kayleigh finished the cycle, then turned and walked to the core where her techno wizardry would thrive under her oversight.

Diana led her agents down the long tunnel to the parking garage and they piled into two new SUVs. With the manpower and the extra equipment they'd been able to purchase lately, they needed to upgrade their carrying capacity.

The team eased through the light nighttime traffic. It was too late for the dinner rush but early enough that they would miss the traffic after the end of theatre performances. Their route took them through the cultural center of town to the far side of the warehouse and wholesale district. They parked a couple of blocks away and piled out of the cars.

"Final comms check." Affirmatives followed from everyone, including Rath and Kayleigh. She circled to the rear of the SUV and raised the hatch. In addition to the hardpoints to hold their rifles and stun guns, each car carried several backpacks filled with situational gear. She retrieved one with a stencil of a grapnel on it and put it on. Her rifle followed. They'd decided as a group that the stun gun straps were more annoying than useful, so it was the last thing she picked up to carry. It would also be the first thing discarded when things turned hot.

BAM Pittsburgh gathered around her. Tony and Cara were calm, Rath's three-foot form bounced in anticipation, and the two newcomers looked both nervous and excited. "Kayleigh, are we good to go as planned?"

"Affirmative. The east wall is your best bet for the climb. There is no activity visible through the windows, but thermal scan shows beings on each of the four floors—and not only Kilomea. Smaller forms, too." A schematic of the structure with the heat sources overlaid appeared in her glasses, and Diana scanned it. The figures were in motion, so it was an unreliable source of planning data for anything other than raw numbers at that moment. She gathered Rath and Sloan with a gesture and led them to the building a block away. On a cross street a little further north, the other three agents walked toward the front entrance.

Their dark shirts, pants, and boots blended with the night as Diana carefully avoided the pools of illumination cast by the dim streetlights along their path. Kayleigh had modified the police stun guns by painting them black and reducing the weight with cutouts and replacement parts. She'd promised to redesign them from the ground up, but time hadn't allowed it yet.

*One more reason to stay, my pretty.*

The SWAT versions were meant to be a visible deterrent. BAM Pittsburg generally couldn't afford such luxuries.

They arrived at the building within minutes. Kayleigh had selected a good approach angle and small dark windows stood out at regular intervals. Since the tech hadn't provided visuals through them of the room inside, they were probably shaded or blocked. Their ascent would remain undetected. Diana unclipped her backpack straps, pulled the bag free from the rest of her gear, and set it on the ground. She felt behind her to ensure that the Ruger and Bowie knife were where they were supposed to be. When she turned, the team's Face had already knelt to remove the bipod base, launch tube, and rocket-shaped grapnel from the pack.

The device was modeled after an army mortar. All one had to do was drop the projectile into the tube, where it would strike a firing pin that launched it at an angle defined by the cylinder's positioning. The "bomb" was rather different than standard in that its body was mostly filled with compressed air for thrust and it had outer panels that would fall away once the onboard sensors detected downward motion. A final burst of air would deploy the five tines that would, hopefully, catch the edge of the building and hold. The grapple line was thin and strong enough to support a person's weight. Unfortunately, for safety reasons, they would have to ascend one at a time.

Sloan positioned the tube and locked it in place. Rath dropped the round in, and it rocketed into the air. The party only had one backup. If they missed twice, they would be forced to retrieve the other backpack from Cara's car, which would be a humiliation impossible to live down on top of a waste of precious minutes. Diana breathed a sigh of relief when she heard the tines catch on the rooftop.

"Good positioning, Sloan. Good firing, Rath." She pressed the stud on her glasses to increase the size of the window that displayed the drone feed. The roof was still clear.

*Haptics in the gloves would be useful. I'm totally adding it to the list.*

The troll scampered up the line, as agile as always. He barely needed the knots that had been tied to aid ascent. Diana followed, and Sloan climbed after her. They would have taken the skylight under normal circumstances, but this building had invested in bulletproof glass, which would take too much effort to break and also make too much noise.

*So, the stairs it is.*

They opened the door that guarded their route carefully and checked first with the fiber optic cameras to be sure there were no surprises on the other side. It stood unlocked, untrapped, and unguarded. Sloan whispered, "Deploying crawler," and stuck a small piece of metal to the sloped ceiling. Articulated legs unfolded, and the device began to move. Its miniature feet stuck to the roof with a form of technology she couldn't even begin to understand. Kayleigh had tried to explain once, but the agent's eyes had glazed over, which prompted Cara to advise, "Think of it as a robot spider."

*A cute, tiny, creepy, artificially-intelligent arachnid.*

The feed from the machine replaced the drone feed in her glasses, courtesy of the low-profile repeaters buckled to each of their belts. The signal boosters were Kayleigh's design. She had huffed about being useless during missions and rejected the bulky backpacks that ARES traditionally wore when they needed more wireless juice. She'd promised to find a better means to secure them for the future, but for now, they were no more distracting than a flashlight would be.

The crawler scuttled down the stairs and into the main room on the top floor. A mixture of human and Kilomea were too busy looting the cases to notice the tiny device. Diana pressed the stud on her glove to speak. "We have extras down there. Humans. Magic status unknown. Right now, they're bagmen." Each of the humans held the bags open as their larger counterparts used their massive hands to sweep as many gems and pieces of jewelry as possible into the sacks.

*It seems backward to make the smaller ones carry the heavy stuff.*

A double click matched the blink from the small LED that represented Cara in the far upper left of her display. Diana led her people carefully down the stairs and made sure to confirm the crawler's initial analysis of a lack of traps. When nothing magical or technological was found, she guided her team to the door and set up positions.

*No sentries means they're confident. Or Arrogant.*

She tapped her glasses to trigger a thirty-second countdown in her team's fields of vision. The ground unit would breach a minute after she started the action upstairs. As long as they followed the plan, the criminals on the lower floors would be distracted by the ruckus above in the moments before Cara's group broke through.

*Confusion to our enemies. The more distracted they are, the better.*

They struck at zero. Diana led the way with a flashbang that clattered on the floor before it detonated. She fired at the nearest human on the right with her stun gun and dropped him easily. Sloan followed, his shots directed at the opposite side of the room. Rath dashed up the middle toward another human in sensory overload and jabbed the shock batons into his spine. The man collapsed and a dose of sedative finished the job and rendered the man unconscious. Once Diana had disabled her first target, she smiled at one of the Kilomea, put him in her sights, and pulled the trigger. The huge creature grinned at her and she remembered too late what Warden Murphy had said about their resistance to the drone-mounted stun guns.

*Great memory, Sheen.*

The comms were on voice activation during action, so she didn't have to hit the toggle to remind the others of that weakness. She shoved the weapon at the Kilomea as she passed her warning along the network. The instinctive block the giant imposed gave her time to raise her M4. She discharged a triple-tap at center mass and followed it with two at head level. All five found their mark, and the giant dropped.

Sloan's rifle chattered noisily as he released a volley at another Kilomea. He wounded it with the first burst, then scuttled right to clear the obstacle it had ducked behind and completed the assault. Rath had climbed on top of one of the display cases and currently pounded his batons on a human who held his hands protectively over his head. A staccato sequence of body blows was punctuated by snaps from the shock elements, and the man fell.

The final Kilomea on the level barreled into the combat zone from a back area. Diana fired, but he dodged and rolled to his left. The party had engaged in long discussions about the creatures' combat intuitions, which seemed to give them a better than usual chance to dodge incoming attacks. Kayleigh put it down to their history as hunters, while Rath thought it was probably long experience. Diana decided it was something in the middle—instincts combined with play that doubled as practice. Whatever the truth might have been, he soon found his feet and raced at her, a chair held in front of him as a shield.

*A chair? Seriously?*

Diana let her rifle fall and extended her arms to pull the furniture to the left with her telekinesis. When the giant yanked it to the right to counter the move, she released her grasp. The resulting backlash from the overcompensation threw his balance off, and the force blast she conjured splintered the chair. The next struck him directly in the face. For a moment, he hovered in the air like a cartoon before gravity reasserted itself over his senseless form and hauled him into a thunderous impact.

Kayleigh's voice crackled in her ear. "Get ready. They're on the move toward the top and there are more of them than we thought. They must have worn thermal dampeners."

She sighed. "So, a trap?"

"Trap," the tech confirmed.

Rath clapped. "So, are we going in?"

Diana grinned. "It's about time you watched *Serenity,* Rath."

The troll shrugged. "I get excitable about choice. Like to keep my options open."

*That was a decent impression, accent and all.*

She laughed. "Onward, people." In her HUD, the counter for Cara's team clicked down to zero.

## CHAPTER FIFTEEN

Cara gestured, and the SWAT unit swung the outer door open. The BAM team waited for a moment in case the enemy had planted surprises in the entrance, but no explosions or traps activated. She led the way cautiously inside. Anik followed behind her and Tony brought up the rear. They held their stun rifles at the ready as they cleared the entry floor. The lobby contained no interesting features beyond a small door to what was assuredly a tiny deathtrap elevator and an unmanned guard desk in the center. She looked over the top and noticed that the security monitors were powered down.

"Cara, you're clear to the second level, but I see considerable activity up there," Kayleigh warned. "The drone's at a bad angle to identify where people are horizontally, and the other one is still too far away to help. I estimate a minimum of five and as many as eight up there, and at least three big boys. Or girls. Whatever." While the other members of the team always came across as amped up over the comms, the tech generally sounded annoyed by anything that limited her omniscience.

*Good attitude, blondie.*

The ex-Marshall led the way up the staircase one quiet footfall at a time. Their training had ensured that she would be alert for most traps the thieves might try to set. Her ears strained for any sound that could betray the enemy's movements and the sharp turn at the top didn't fill her with confidence. She shifted the stun gun to her left hand and pulled and primed a flashbang with her right. "I'll bank it off the wall. If it goes wrong, head down the stairs. Fast."

She threw the canister with as much force as she could muster and aimed for the surface several feet above the end of the railing. The grenade flew true and bounced off to careen out of sight. She rounded the corner in the same moment that it detonated.

Her glasses and earplugs protected her from the blast, and she'd trained to ignore the concussion. With two quick shots, she eliminated the humans closest to her. The stun gun did its work effectively and efficiently, and she took care of the others beyond the initial group. Anik moved to her left, Tony to her right, and the two men fired on the remaining human targets. The enemy recovered quickly, however, and waved wands that dissipated the incoming energy.

*Damn it.*

"We have mages down here." Cara tossed her stun gun far enough out of the way that she wouldn't trip on it. She drew the Glock and fired in a smooth motion, aiming at the heart of the witch nearest her. The woman conjured a shield, but the triple burst of anti-magic bullets plowed through it. She staggered under the impacts but didn't fall and immediately waved her wand.

*What the—*

Cara dodged, but the lightning struck her a glancing blow. She summoned a growl as one of her magic deflectors went dark and shifted her aim to a wizard already engaged with Anik. It was a long shot, but she managed to put the round intended for his chest into his leg as he flung himself aside. There was no time for follow up, though, and she hastily holstered her pistol to prepare to meet the Kilomea who now attacked in earnest.

In the meantime, Tony had worked his way quietly around to the right. He found an angle on the witch attacking Cara, discharged his stun gun, and caught his target squarely. The electrical current overloaded her undefended nervous system as well as it would have done on a normal human, and he grinned in satisfaction. A small desk rocketed toward his head and he yelped and dropped to the floor. He shoved himself to his feet again in time to see the Kilomea who'd thrown the furniture bare his teeth in a fanged grin and charge.

Cara judged that there wouldn't be enough time to raise her rifle before her own adversary reached her, so she chose a strategy of surprise instead. As her foe neared, she took two steps toward him and leapt forward and to the side to thrust her right foot on the top edge of a display case. She pushed off to reach shoulder level with her attacker and struck at his neck. Still in motion, she used their combined momentum to rotate around him and settle onto his shoulders. She rammed her shock gloves into his neck and ground them in as he howled in pain. He fell to his knees, and she lurched ahead into a tumble as his face planted itself in the wooden floor with the snap of crunching bones and cartilage.

Tony's response was more straightforward. He dropped his stun rifle and fired his pistol from the hip to deliver a triangle of bullets into his adversary's face. The behemoth dropped like a puppet whose strings had been cut. Tony shoved the pistol into its holster and bent to retrieve the non-lethal weapon again.

Anik took the more direct approach and raised his rifle to track one of the females. She was a little shorter than her kin, but her mass was equally as deadly as she bore down on him. He squeezed the trigger in a smooth rhythm and tracked her as she tried to dodge. He missed three times before he found his mark and maintained the assault as she fell. Once she was dead, he swung the weapon to the center of the room in search of his next target, but the remaining enemies flashed past on their way to the stairs. He managed a short, "Hey!" as they fled before an outstretched arm from one of the enemy made him stumble. Both he and Tony fired, but shields activated to deflect their attacks.

The two men hurried forward, but Cara blocked their pursuit hastily. "It's too easy. Something's not right. Kayleigh, what's going on in here?"

The tech replied instantly. "They seem to have congregated a floor up, with more on the one above that. I have the second drone triangulating, but if they're rocking thermal protection, I can't be certain of the numbers.

There are beings present on both levels, for sure. Some in the rooms and some near the stairs."

Cara nodded. "So, it's still a trap."

"Definitely," Diana agreed. "Let's turn it around on them. You try to draw them this time. If any from the fourth floor head your way, we'll attack from behind."

"Affirmative, boss. Wait one." She turned to her team. "Okay, Tony, ditch the stun gun. Anik, give me your anti-magic pistol mag." He complied, and she slotted it into her firearm. "Tony and I are on magicals. Anik, you hose down any Kilomeas who rear their ugly head. When we need to reload, sonic grenades go in. If you're in doubt, throw pepper or flashbangs if you have 'em, but call out anything other than the noisemakers."

She crept forward, knelt beside the stairs, and fed her fiber-optic camera around one of the poles of the banister. The feed opened in her glasses to reveal that once again, their route to the higher floor was uncontested. She let the camera retract into its housing under her forearm guard and waved her team ahead. They tiptoed up several steps, and her mind was already plotting the trajectory of the next grenade bank-shot when something poked warningly at the place where her spine met her skull. She stopped and peered in all directions as she tried to identify what had triggered her fear instinct

When she finally saw it, she was amazed she'd noticed at all. The difference in lighting on the landing was so subtle that it would have been entirely too easy to miss. Something clearly lingered in the way of the light from around the corner. She backed away and whispered, "It looks like an ambush ahead at the entrance to the third floor."

"Affirmative," Diana replied. "You got this?"

Cara laughed softly. "Oh, yeah, we've got this. Demolition man is in the house." She turned to Anik. "It's time to earn your keep. We'll go up together and I'll snake a camera around the corner. If it's an obstruction, you blow it up. If it's criminals, we both shoot 'em. Any questions?"

He grinned. "If it's a criminal, can I still blow him up?"

"I'll go with definitely and totally yes on that one."

"Excellent."

Tony sighed. "I'm always forgotten. That's me. I guess I'll hang out down here and shop for something nice for my future wife."

Cara crooked a finger at him. "You have the toughest job of all. If these are wizards, you'll need to leave cover and shoot them, since I'll most likely be on the floor. We have to assume they'll see the camera, even though they probably won't."

He drew his backup gun with his off-hand to join the Glock he held in the other. "Okay, let's do this." The former cop had already proven himself to be a master of the dual wield on the shooting range. Cara's pride still smarted from how easily he'd outstripped her.

*Maybe our resident cowboy should carry two pistols, plus the Ruger.*

She crawled forward with Anik at her side. He carried shaped charges in each hand, ready to deploy against anything they might encounter. She slithered as close as she could and slid the camera around the edge. A hasty blockade had been created by a desk wedged diagonally with chairs packed into the gaps. Fortunately, the corner of the desk also blocked the view of their approach from below, so Anik was able to wriggle closer and place the explosives. He slid back with a grin and whispered, "I hope they like splinters because they're gonna get some."

The timers counted down and the barrier disintegrated. They barreled around the corner to find that the enemy was smarter than they had expected. Wizards and witches had raised shields in preparation for the incursion and none of them had taken any damage. Worse, they had positioned a rifleman at each side. Cara slid to avoid the incoming bullets and retargeted her pistol on the nearest gunman. Unfortunately, this wasted precious anti-magic rounds.

Tony was the next to react, but his precipitous action was badly timed. The rounds from the other rifleman struck his vest and he tumbled awkwardly down the stairs. Anik fired half a carbine magazine and removed one man from the picture before the wizard beside him could raise a shield to protect him. The demolitions expert traversed his rifle across the enemy on full auto until the weapon clicked empty, but the magazine was filled with regular bullets, which were easily deflected by the mages.

Cara took advantage of their distraction to plant a fist in the face of the nearest wizard. He recoiled from the blow and stumbled dazedly. She immediately followed with a kick that propelled him into the witch beside him.

"Take them, Anik," she shouted as she ducked under a punch from one of the Kilomea before the even-larger brute beside him kicked her. Her ribs cracked under the blow, and she was instantly thankful for the Kevlar that protected them from shattering. She literally bounced off the floor an instant before she impacted the far wall and lay stunned as the room spun around her. The closest of the two giants advanced and the other lunged at Anik.

The look on his face was pure panic as he was buried under a mountain of alien creature. If the situation hadn't been so dire, Cara would have laughed. As it was, she did the only thing she could do. She yelled and thrust the hand that wasn't trapped beneath her at her Kilomea. Bolts of shaped flame clustered in the foe's chest. Her vision sharpened enough that she could see his shocked expression as the darts drilled into and through him, then emerged on the far side to embed themselves in the ceiling, where they began to smolder. She had enough time for three final thoughts as she fell into darkness.

*Bad angle. Fire. That's not good.*

---

Anik's last thought before impact was, *Holy hell, he's immense.* Pain prompted a string of curses before his brain started working again. The monster had rolled him toward the landing, and the demolitions expert now had the perfect position. He yelled, "Watch out, Tony!" and kicked the Kilomea's knee as the brute climbed to his feet. The unexpected strike forced his adversary to drop forward, and he thrust his heel in the giant's thigh to finish the job. The colossus bellowed in surprise as gravity took its inevitable course. Tony avoided the enemy, raced past Anik, and scowled as he brought his weapons to bear.

The pistols barked as he aimed at the wizards and

fired through each of their shields. No blood flowed, although they fell in a sprawled heap. As a former officer, he knew only too well what that meant. They wore Kevlar, which wasn't the best news. Still, the impact provided enough of a distraction for him to stalk forward and drive a boot into each of their heads and take them out of the fight. He jogged away in the direction Cara had taken.

Anik eased cautiously around the corner at the top of the stairs. At the bottom, the Kilomea struggled groggily to his feet. The agent smiled as he retrieved a flash bang and a sonic grenade, popped the seal on each, and lobbed them underhanded at his foe. His timing was flawless, and they detonated on impact with the massive creature. The resulting sound stunned the behemoth and he dropped in a heap as the sound blew his eardrums out. Anik thought about finishing the creature, but it was enough to have him out of action.

*For now.*

He staggered into the room and knelt to zip-tie the fallen. Tony had wrangled Cara into a sitting position and helped her to sip a healing potion held in a protective canister. The detonations expert had one on his belt as well, and while they preferred not to waste valuable resources, Diana had told them not to second-guess themselves. If they thought they might need it, they would worry about the consequences later.

Tony and Cara stood together and she cradled her chest. Her breathing seemed a little easier, so she was clearly on the mend. Anik joined them, and the trio walked slowly toward the stairs once more.

Kayleigh's voice crackled over the comms and they startled. "There's a group on the fourth floor. Be careful."

Diana's reply came in a growling tone. "The more the merrier. Move your tails, slackers, or there won't be any left for you."

Tony shook his head and Anik laughed. Cara triggered her mic, which had been knocked offline when she'd struck the wall. "I love you, too, boss. Try not to step on any tripwires."

Diana's response was colorfully crude as they started up the stairs at a jog. Judging by the previous patterns, this floor would probably be the most difficult. Like the boss said, they didn't want to miss out on the fun.

# CHAPTER SIXTEEN

Diana did, in fact, check carefully for traps on the way down. She had watched the feed Kayleigh bounced from Cara's glasses into a window on hers. The blockade was an admirable step in strategy and it also made her cautious. Rath was a step behind on her left and Sloan on the right. They arrived at the main room without meeting opposition, but before she could question this, her bracelet turned ice cold.

*Fuck me. Illusions. Why didn't I anticipate that?*

She shouted, "Pepper!" and hurled a grenade ahead. It bounced off something and detonated. The illusionary wall that concealed the enemy vanished. Three people with rifles opened fire, and she summoned a force shield to protect them from the onslaught. The bullets ricocheted wildly and bounced around the room. The noxious cloud caught a Kilomea, and he choked and hacked as he spun to the rear of their formation. A nearby wizard waved his wand and directed the vapor away from the group.

"We gotta move. Go," Diana commanded and deactivated the shield as Rath and Sloan scattered in opposite directions. The team's undercover officer, who wore a mask to conceal his features, did the smart thing and retreated to the staircase where the angles would provide him a clear firing line while it also afforded him a measure of cover. True to their natures, Diana and Rath charged ahead.

The troll pounded toward the rifleman on the left and a woman with a wand behind him. A flurry of shots spewed viciously, but the diminutive assailant used the wall as a launch pad to become a projectile of his own. The rifleman ducked to avoid him, and Rath grinned. The witch raised her wand level with the living missile in the nick of time, but the force she conjured to deflect him didn't prevent his batons from making contact with her shoulders. At a sharp sizzle and pop, she collapsed, temporarily stunned.

Her defensive maneuver careened the troll toward a Kilomea. The creature opened its arms wide to catch him, and Rath twisted to lead with his legs. The giant grabbed hold as they touched but the strong hands pinched empty air, having barely missed the troll when he shrunk enough to avoid being caught. He grew again quickly and shoved against his assailant's hands, ran up the enormous body, and pushed off once he reached the perfect launching place. He tumbled into a back somersault and had reached five feet in height when he landed heavily. A few moments later, he stood at just over seven and grinned as he blocked the Kilomea's punch. The two opponents were now on a far more even footing.

Diana saw it all in flashes as she battled her own foes. A duo of wizards had unleashed a murderous volley of blasts immediately when her shield fell. The lightning and fire were absorbed by the protective aura of her magic deflectors, which popped rapidly in series.

*Shit. Only one left.*

The attacks forced her to redirect her charge toward the largest Kilomea in the room rather than the rifleman she'd originally targeted. She snatched a pair of grenades without looking, but repeated practice ensured that she had a sonic in her right and a flashbang in the other. She called out as she threw them. "Light and scream out!"

The sound ordnance detonated at the feet of the wizards and rendered them insensate, for a while at least. The Kilomea ahead batted the projectile intended for him away, and it sailed past Rath and into the far corner. In the brief look she had as she tracked the deflected item, it seemed like the two giant creatures took turns to exchange furious punches and blows.

*Surely not. It must be a trick of the light.*

The flashbang distracted the troll's challenger for an instant, and Rath's uppercut catapulted him back to crash onto a display case. Shards of glass sliced through the Kilomea's skin and splinters embedded themselves in various locations on his way to the floor.

One of the towering creatures managed only a step toward Diana before her hands closed on her rifle. A quick check of the sight lines ensured that her allies were out of the way. She flicked the weapon to auto and pulled the trigger. The slugs traced a diagonal from floor level on the left of the creature, peaked at his head, and descended on the opposite side as she yanked the barrel down. She spun and fired on the downed wizards, but one of them had enough power remaining to summon a shield.

Diana ejected the magazine as the Kilomea fell and rammed in a replacement with a blue stripe. She flicked the selector back to single and fired bursts of three into each mage. The lack of blood revealed the same thing Cara had discovered downstairs.

*Kevlar. I hate it when they learn.*

She sighted carefully and put one round into each arm and a single leg on each target. The ammunition was indifferent to the shield the man tried to maintain. She grinned as she fired the last bullet into the thigh of the farthest wizard.

*See, Rodriguez? Sometimes, I get it right.*

When she straightened and sought her next target, there were none to be found. Between the grenades, the troll, and Sloan's meticulously targeted fire, their enemies were all eliminated or disabled. Her sense of triumph was soured a little when she realized that the floor and one wall were burning. "Kayleigh, roll the fire department to this location."

"Already done, boss. PD is on the way, too. Plus, you have a group of news drones outside, so if you don't want your face to be on TV, cover up." A case was currently in progress through the courts to limit the use of the mechanicals by media organizations, but right now, it was more or less a free-for-all. As long as they were authorized to fly the devices, they could put cameras on them and call it news. The Pittsburgh stations hadn't committed any particularly egregious offenses, but she'd heard a story from Las Vegas about drones detailed to constantly track the actions of the Brownstone Agency. Whether this was to celebrate or castigate was still unclear.

*He's so well-known, they could probably release a movie of his fights into the theaters and make millions. And no, I'm not jealous.*

Her inner voice laughed at her, all-knowing, as usual.

*Shut up, you.*

The other crew joined them a moment later. Cara gestured at the flames. "Seriously?" Diana glared at her, but she continued. "The fire I started is *much* more impressive." They shared a tired laugh, which was interrupted by a familiar *whoosh* as a trio of portals materialized.

Three identical witches stepped through the gateways, decked in black tactical gear that looked eerily similar to that which the BAM operatives wore. They cast simultaneously, and the furniture in the room was reduced to debris. Display cabinets transformed into shrapnel. Desks and chairs became flying battering rams. Rath raced toward the stairwell and dodged as best as his larger body would allow while Cara slipped into the descending stairwell. Diana used her telekinesis to protect herself and directed the largest of the projectiles away while she held a barrier in place before Tony, Sloan, and Anik. Fortunately, the three had enough sense to retreat as quickly as possible to avoid putting undue strain on their leader.

Diana scowled as the huge bags of loot elevated and spun into the portals. She attempted to move forward, but two casters kept her pinned down by threatening her team. They shifted positions to maintain a trajectory on the others and forced her to maintain the barrier over the stairwell. She flicked objects at them, but the witches blocked them as easily as she had. It was a stalemate for the moment. The others would be back in the game soon, but until they returned, she could do nothing but defend.

Downed enemies were pulled through the portals one by one. Diana gritted her teeth in frustration until the sharp retort of gunfire sounded, and the witches jerked backward. The team had regrouped, and their anti-magic bullets punched through to impact in Kevlar and other protective plates of the enemy. The first two witches stepped back through the rift. The last nodded at Diana as she retreated through her own. The condescending smirk on her face was the final insult.

The portals collapsed, and they were alone again. Cara stepped beside her. "Who the hell were those guys?"

She shook her head. "Assholes."

The other woman gave a single bark of mirth. "Sure, but new ones, right? They didn't look the same as the ones we've faced before."

Diana turned and waved for the team to follow her to the stairs, where Rath waited. She handed him the vest he'd discarded when he grew, and he nodded in appreciation as he shrank to the appropriate size again.

"Kayleigh, are we clear to exit the roof?"

The tech's voice replied after a brief interval. "Keep your masks on, but yes, there's no opposition."

She removed her black mask from the pouch at her belt and put it on and watched her team do the same, sans Sloan, since his hadn't been removed in the battle. Satisfied, she focused on Cara. "Yeah, I'd agree that they aren't familiar. They seem disconnected from the Remembrance."

"So, we have two teams of magical enemies now. Awesome."

Sloan grinned. "The more the merrier. We'll have the bounty cash for the mobile armory in no time."

Diana sighed and gestured around the room. "Maybe we should simply break into high-end stores. It would be easier and faster."

The other woman whacked her on the shoulder. "We're the good guys, boss. Remember?"

She slapped a hand dramatically on her forehead. "Right, right. Sorry, I forgot for a minute."

Rath, who had remained silent through the whole adventure, came over to stand beside her. His voice was deep and breathy when he spoke. "I find your lack of faith…disturbing." He maintained his Darth Vader impersonation as the team ascended.

By the time they reached the roof, Diana had pushed through the frustration and renewed her determination.

*I don't care how many gangs of scumbags there are. This is my town, and you'll all go down, one at a time if need be.*

# CHAPTER SEVENTEEN

The team was already assembled in the fifth-floor conference room when Diana and Bryant arrived just after two in the afternoon. His brown hair was carefully combed, and his suit conformed to the toned muscles of his body. She moved immediately to the coffeemaker, and he took a seat at the head of the table. Only Rath and Max were missing. The duo had chosen to stay at home, doubtless to rest in preparation for some unknown adventure.

Cara looked exhausted. The healing potion had done its work but at the cost of her body's energy stores being drastically drained to hasten the recovery.

*We have to build up our energy potion supply, too.*

Nylotte created and acquired supplies on their behalf at a steady pace, but as their tasks increased, so did their needs.

*Damn. I forgot. I need to take some deflector crystals to her next time.*

Sometimes, Diana thought the Drow merely requested things to keep her on a permanent scavenger hunt.

Bryant exchanged greetings with the others, and Tony introduced him to the two new members of BAM Pittsburgh. Nods were traded, but the room was uncharacteristically reserved. Bryant's serious demeanor and her own combined to cast a pall over the space. She sat and ceded precedence to him with a wave of her hand.

He cleared his throat. "First, let me say excellent work on the response to the break-in. You did an effective job of dealing with the threat, and the fire damage was minimal. The merchandise was insured and no innocents were harmed. All in all, it was a suitable deployment."

Tony bumped Cara's shoulder with his own. "Did you hear that? Bryant said you're not innocent." He raised and lowered his eyebrows suggestively at her.

She rolled her eyes. "Dream on, Lothario. You wouldn't survive it."

Bryant's lips twitched—only a touch, but it was good to see. "The bad news is that other adventures last night didn't go nearly as well. There were several attacks, and we think the timing is too coincidental to be anything other than intentional. ARES DC, Hartford, and Buffalo were also targeted."

Kayleigh spoke for them all when she said, "Is DC okay? Is everyone all right?" Her hands were clenched tightly, and the nails dug into her palms as her knuckles paled.

Bryant shook his head. "DC has some wounded, but nothing worse. They were attacked during a response to a break-in similar to yours. Hartford is our newest location. They had only a few operatives and as a result, they have one dead and one missing. They were gathered at a restaurant, and civilians were hurt as well. No fatalities are among them yet, but a few are in critical condition."

Blood drained from the faces around the room. The pattern was clear, and he soon confirmed it.

"Buffalo was wiped out. They struck the base and killed everyone in it, then blew up the installation."

Diana barely contained the outrage that burned violently within. Cara wasn't nearly so subtle. She was a soldier, and soldiers didn't take losing their own lightly. It was a sentiment her boss related to well. She saw the same tension in every member of her team except Kayleigh, who was too stunned to let the anger settle.

"Were the other bases secret?" Sloan asked.

Bryant nodded. "The same model we've used here is implemented everywhere."

"So how did they find out?"

"Unknown and it's under investigation. The existence of the ARES locations was known only to the Army Corps of Engineers and their superiors, our agents, and the oversight council. There's no reason to think anyone in that chain would reveal it deliberately, as we've all been vetted to hell and back."

Sloan nodded. "Technology? Magic?"

"It could be either." He shrugged. "We're looking into all possibilities."

"Including those who have been vetted to hell and back?"

"Yes." Bryant sighed heavily. The cost of distrusting those above him was clear on his face. "The rollout is paused for the time being. It's too dangerous right now.

We'll abandon Buffalo for the short term and focus on shoring up Hartford, instead. You seem able to take care of yourselves."

The team's heads turned toward Diana, who nodded. "Yes, I'd say we have it more or less under control."

His shifted his gaze to Kayleigh. "Taggart would like you to stay here for a while longer if that's okay with you. There's not enough good science to go around."

She nodded numbly. Diana couldn't muster the effort to feel smug, though. The situation was too sobering, and it showed on everyone's faces. One thing was certain.

*This hurts. We need to find these fuckers and put them out of business permanently.*

Bryant looked grimly at his watch. "Diana and I have to conference with DC. If you have questions, text me."

---

The core awoke as they exited the elevator and strode into its sensor range. The remainder of the floor stayed dark as the monitors flickered to life and screensaver art bounced around, courtesy of Kayleigh's warped sense of humor. A series of toasters with wings flapped with every second of "air time." Diana pressed a few buttons on the center table's virtual interface and an array of displays switched to images of a stylized, many-pointed star. She and Bryant took position in front of the camera, and at the appointed second, the logos faded one by one to be replaced with people.

Senator Aaron Finley was in the far left with an office, presumably his, in the background. He appeared both angry and upset. The next displayed a person Diana hadn't met, but Bryant had shown her his picture. Stan Dykstrom was the head of ARES in Hartford. A butterfly bandage held a cut closed at the corner of his left eye. Heavy bags sagged under his darkened eyes.

*He probably spent the night in the hospital, either for himself, for the team, or for the civilians wounded in the attack. It sucks to be in charge, sometimes.*

The third monitor showed Carson Taggart, who wore as ferocious an expression as Diana had ever seen from him. She'd known the steel in his spine had to be there, but his glare provided confirmation of the fact. Her first thought was that she was glad it wasn't aimed at her.

Finally, the fourth display was suddenly and unexpectedly filled with the frowning face of the Vice President of the United States. Diana snapped reflexively to attention, and Bryant did the same beside her. His deep voice sounded exactly like he always did on television.

"On behalf of the President, and of the ARES oversight council, I want you to understand that we share your sorrow. This calculated attack must be answered and shall be answered. The public may never be aware of the sacrifices made for their benefit by your comrades, but we know, and we will remember. You have our support. And as SAC Taggart has been assured, you have virtually unlimited latitude in your response to this deliberate provocation. Stay safe, and kick some tail for your fallen, for your country, and for your planet." He nodded, and his screen faded to darkness.

*Well. That's not something you see every day.*

Everyone held their breath and stance as if the man

might suddenly reappear, but after several seconds, they relaxed to greater or lesser degrees, based on their positions. Finley appeared anxious, Taggart furious, and the remainder of them moved into some version of parade rest. The head of ARES frowned before speaking.

"So, there are innumerable questions we need to address. First, is this one group or multiple groups? Second, how did they find out about the Buffalo base? Third, what's their endgame?" He paused, then added, "What have I left out?"

Bryant was the quickest to respond. "What's their middle game? We have to assume this is the start of something, or at least near the beginning. The attack on the Cube was the opening salvo—the Remembrance saying, 'we're here, fear us.' If this is them, it's an escalation, but I can't imagine that they've shown their entire strategy yet."

Diana and Dykstrom both nodded. Finley squirmed. Taggart's eyes darted to where the screen would have shown on his monitors, then asked, "Senator?"

The council go-between leaned back in his chair and sighed. The camera focus pulsed once before it brought him properly into view. "We have a systemic problem here. They messed with our supply lines. They went after our prison. Now, they've attacked our people directly. This is somewhere beyond business and into the personal if you know what I mean. What I don't understand is why. We haven't been that big a thorn in their side yet, have we? How are they so aware of us? Could this all be fallout from the attempt to kidnap the ambassador?"

Diana blinked. The political dimensions of the equation had been temporarily swamped by operational concerns, but she now saw his line of thought. There was no reason to think the enemy was working on only one front.

Bryant stroked his chin, and the sound of bristles scraping filled the room. "So what you're suggesting is that this could be the tactical side of a political strategy?"

The Senator nodded. "Or, at the very least, they intertwine. Otherwise, the attack on the ambassador seems unconnected, and that simply isn't probable."

Taggart frowned. "That makes sense. So, let's add that to the list." He sighed and straightened, his expression resolute. "Okay, here's the plan. First, we beef up security. Second, we collect intelligence. Third, we find these bastards and knock their teeth down their throats." He nodded in approval of his own decisions. "Get to it. Daily conferences at oh-eight-hundred until further notice. Tech discussions to follow at nine, so coordinate with your people. Talk to you tomorrow."

The monitors died as ARES DC, who had hosted the meeting, killed the connections. Diana turned to face Bryant and leaned on the display table. "So, security and intel."

He nodded. "Kayleigh can work on establishing deeper access into the local sources. I'm reasonably sure that the Vice President just gave us permission to do whatever we feel we need to do."

"It's fun being off the books."

"At least until we get arrested."

She rewarded him with a laugh

"Anyway, you might want to put a little more oversight on the people upstairs. They provide decent cover, but they could be a liability too," he noted.

Diana nodded.

*Like I've said all along*

"Have the Kemanas local to the attacks been alerted?"

"Yep, at levels higher than ours." Bryant scratched his chin, a gesture that now seemed almost permanent as his mind worked.

She realized she'd never seen him with stubble before.

*It looks good on him.*

"Have Tony talk to Warden Murphy. Make sure the Cube has it all together. I won't have a chance to meet with her this trip." Diana nodded again. "And get your Face out there. It's time for him to earn his pay."

"Hitting on women in bars?" She grinned at the memory of her first sight of Bryant as DC's Face tried to pry her and Lisa apart and failed miserably in the attempt.

He smiled in response. "Only if the situation absolutely requires it." He checked his watch and sighed. "I have a few hours before I have to hit the rack to get out of here in the morning. Dinner?"

"I wouldn't miss it for the world, BC."

## CHAPTER EIGHTEEN

Sloan Woodhouse walked along Liberty Avenue. His grey hooded sweatshirt and distressed jeans allowed him to be merely a body in the crowd of people who went about their daily lives. His hair was unwashed, only finger-combed out of his face, and he looked sloppier than usual. Solid work boots were imperfectly tied, and a chain dangled at his right hip to connect his wallet to a belt loop.

He kept his identity in mind and reaffirmed it with each step.

*Tommy Ketchum, nickname Ketch, grew up poor on the north side, eleventh-grade dropout. Good with locks and high places. Muscle with added skills, basically.*

Everything about him had been altered enough to ensure that no one could connect him to his real identity. A clever lift in his boot altered his walk, and the several days of scruff with a little product to make his eyebrows wilder than normal altered his face. The baggy clothes hid his body. The only thing that wouldn't ring true was his lack of tattoos, but he'd claim to be allergic to the dyes if asked.

He lived in a run-down hotel on a cash-only basis arranged with the person behind the desk, strictly off the books. It was less than glamorous but gave "Ketch" a reason to be hungry for work and connections, all of which he would need to infiltrate the right group.

Kayleigh's deep dive into the PD's surveillance system had brought quick results. They'd identified more low-level operatives in the days after their restrictions had been eased, and Sloan now headed to a meeting with one of them. He'd cultivated random connections where he could since his arrival, and this man had turned out to have an in with another group they were tracking.

If he played his cards right, he could be on the cusp of getting in with the group that had opposed them in the first place. He also might be wasting a whole lot of time on someone who couldn't get him connected at all. That was the problem with undercover work—it was notoriously unpredictable. But over multiple rounds of drinks, his target had ranted about the unfairness of being a non-magical in a gang that included people with power. That alone made the connection worth pursuing.

He pushed into the dive bar, one of many hidden in this section of town, and approached his contact, who was in the center of a gathering of friends. They shook and bumped fists, and he waved at the bartender for his usual. He had a good tolerance for alcohol, which gave him an edge against most of the criminal element he met in bars. By the time they were sloppy, he was only slightly buzzed.

*Clean living. And a hell of a lot of genetic luck.*

In truth, everything about him made him right for undercover work. His magic, his ability to connect with people, and his skill at adopting others' mannerisms were all natural. They'd merely required refining. His trainers said he would have been a great actor had he chosen that path.

*I probably should have. The pay would be better, anyway. And there'd be marginally less risk of getting killed on the job.*

He took a long drink of his beer—Iron City, the local brew—and stood on the sidelines as his contact and friends competed at darts. Sloan suppressed a smile at the way they all dressed in the same jeans and hoodies he wore. It reminded him of high school in a way. Considering how well they threw, it was obvious that they knew how to control their alcohol intake.

*That's promising.*

Eventually, he was challenged and threw a poor game, only partly on purpose. His punishment was buying the next round. He did so cheerfully, and they moved into the back area of the bar, then through an unmarked door and into a very small room with a card table and four rickety chairs.

His contact, Teddy no-last-name-just-Teddy, motioned for him to take a seat and claimed the other side as his own. His features were thin and gaunt, but his aim had been true, which showed dexterity and potential strength. Two others filled the remaining seats, and the last man leaned against the wall, most likely in an attempt to look menacing. If so, he failed badly. The thug looked more like a teenager, and the metal studs over his eyes didn't argue against the possibility.

Teddy leaned forward. "Ketch, we have a thing tonight that might be good for you."

Sloan nodded. "I need a thing. Is there money in it?"

"Some. But more importantly, it's a chance to show what you're made of."

"I'm not here for a fucking audition, Teddy."

The man raised his hands. Like the rest of him, they seemed prematurely aged. Their research had put him in his mid-forties, but his grizzled gray hair and beard suggested at least a decade more. A lifetime of smoking had contributed to the harsh texture of his face, and his nose had clearly been broken several times. Sloan's power had flashed on him at their first meeting. He already knew Teddy's almost skeletal thinness was a result of a chronic illness he kept from his friends but which never strayed far from his mind. If the dip into his thoughts hadn't also revealed his opinions on people who differed from him in any way, Sloan might have felt bad for him.

Teddy smirked. "Settle, bruh. It's all good. It's not an audition, more of a...rite of passage. That's what it is."

Sloan scratched his stubble. "Well, that's a different story, sure. I can get behind that. What are we doing?"

"A little breaking, a little entering, and a little taking from those who have way too much."

"Sounds like fun. When?"

Teddy smiled. "In a while. Before we talk about that, Mur had a question he wanted to ask you."

Sloan shifted in his chair to face the man on his right. They didn't have a file on him yet, although he had been a person of interest since the first time they'd met a few days before. Mur was a large man, more muscle than fat, but definitely had some of each hidden by his baggy clothes. He spoke slowly, which grated on the Face's nerves.

"So, why should we let you run with us? Teddy likes you, but he can be stupid sometimes." The thin man scowled, and Mur laughed it off in a way that showed he'd clearly meant it as an insult.

Sloan's talent could usually be counted on in situations like this, and it didn't disappoint. Mur's real concern was whether or not "Ketch" would break and run if they ran into a tussle.

"Well, Mur, the truth is I have skills that you can use. But, most of all, it seems like you need more muscle. No offense to the guys in the room. And I love smashing teeth in. It's good for all of us."

The chair groaned ominously under Mur's weight as he leaned back.

*One push and he's over. He'd probably crack his head open. Punch Teddy in the face, an elbow to the moron to my left, and it's even odds.*

He hadn't lied. Fighting was one of the things he most enjoyed, but that came second behind his undercover work, which he lived for. Mur grinned suddenly and slapped a palm on the table. "Okay, you're in for tonight. Make it through, and you have a place with us after."

The bald man nodded at Teddy, who poked Sloan on the shoulder. "The fun kicks off at midnight, which gives us time for one more drink. You're buying, new guy."

Sloan grinned. As he approached the bar, he made sure the recording device they'd disguised as his watch was working properly. The second hand still moved, which meant all was well.

*Evidence is good. Undiscovered information is better.*

Access to the higher-ups in the organization, though. That's what the game was all about.

They drove a beat-up van to the location, an antique store nestled in the fairly ritzy Shadyside business district. It was closed, of course, had windows that looked like bulletproof glass, and sported a clearly reinforced door. A dark and narrow alley ran beside it. It stretched about a person and a half wide, so Mur would have had to go in sideways. However, only Teddy preceded him, and no one trailed. They made it about three-quarters of the way down when the thin man pointed up. Sloan followed the gesture and saw a small window above them.

"That used to be an apartment, I think," Teddy whispered. "Now, it's a good access point. There's probably a locked door between, but the blueprints at the county office show that the two floors connect. Easy peasy. We go up, we come down, and we open the front entrance from the inside."

Sloan frowned. "Cameras? There have to be cameras in a place like this, right?"

His partner in crime shook his head and grinned. "Nope. The folks around here are against surveillance, so there's nothing on the street. They fought the police about it and won. That wasn't so smart for them, but it's convenient for us. A system's hooked up inside, but we'll be in and out before it matters." He handed Sloan a ski mask, and the agent pulled it on as Teddy donned his own. The skinny man shrugged out of the rope looped diagonally across his torso. "We did some recon. It's climbable, as long as you're good. Are you good?"

*Ah, the first challenge. Sure, let's play.*

"Better than good. I'm like Spider Man, man."

Teddy grinned and handed him the line. Sloan knotted it twice around his waist and ensured that the excess dangled behind him. Teddy extended a pistol to him.

*Damn.*

There were a million arguments against taking it, most of them involving him having to use it or being tied to a weapon used in a previous crime.

*Ketch wouldn't worry about that, though. He'd see it as a sign of trust.*

He smiled, took it, and sighted down the barrel with a grin he thought might have won an award. The weight felt right for it to be fully loaded.

As he looked over his shoulder at Teddy to thank him, he had a flash of insight. The man was thinking about how the gun wouldn't fire, so handing it over was safe, even if Ketch turned out to be untrustworthy. Sloan suppressed his grin.

*I can work with that.*

He shoved the weapon in the back of his belt above where the knots in the rope hung and reached for the decorative bricks that made a pattern on the wall.

His contact hadn't lied. It was an easy climb. The only moment of challenge came when one of the bricks crumbled as he put his foot on it. It wasn't his first ascent of this kind, though, so he compensated easily. When he reached the window, he found it secured with a standard latch that he slid aside with the thin wedge of metal Teddy had provided for the purpose. He opened it and swung himself inside.

The aperture led to a small bathroom that was long

disused and smelled of dust and dirt. He held the rope for the other man to use in his climb, even though he probably didn't need it, and they tied it off to the sink in case they required an exit route later. Teddy took the lead as they padded through the apartment and found the entrance into the shop at the bottom of a straight flight of stairs. It was a standard internal door. His partner bent to pick the lock, and Sloan tapped his shoulder and whispered in his ear. "Alarms?"

Teddy shrugged. "Maybe operational, maybe not. We'll know once we're inside. If there is one and it's only recording, we'll wreck it. If it's not working, that's more time to collect stuff. Either way, open the front, take whatever looks valuable, and get the hell out."

Sloan nodded, and the other man pushed the door. No sirens sounded, and they found the alarm system only covered the doors on the first floor that led to the outside. It was an easy task to dummy the electrical feeds with a battery at the panel and snip the wires that were designed to carry the signal to the police.

With the job complete, they opened the entrance for the others in the group. The three rushed inside with Mur in the lead. Low whispers followed as the big man pointed his cronies at the left and right of the room and waved to indicate that Teddy and Sloan should join him in the back.

An office in the rear held a giant freestanding safe that doubtless weighed more than a thousand pounds.

*Damn. They must have had to reinforce the floor for that thing.*

The large man dragged a chair over and sat in front of the combination lock. Sloan expected him to produce a stethoscope or a drill, given the way the night was going, but he spun the dial several times, pulled the latch, and the door swung ponderously open.

He didn't have to hide his surprise. "How did you do that?"

"It pays to have friends, Ketch. And as you can see, we're good friends to have."

He withdrew an item wrapped in a thick cloth and placed it on the counter behind him. It was clearly something of great value based on the way he treated it, and there was a clean route to the outer door.

*Uh-huh. I'm not an amateur, guys, and I'd have to be an idiot to grab it and run. Or did you think I would try to shoot you with my dysfunctional pistol? Even if I didn't know it was a dud, I wouldn't trust a weapon from y'all.*

He waited as they cleared the safe, which held a number of other precious items. When they returned to the front, the others carried big duffels filled with all manner of valuables, and the thugs made their escape and loaded the bags in the rear of a van. Before they could enter the vehicle, a police cruiser turned the corner a half-block away. Its roof lights activated, and the siren whooped before a loudspeaker blared, "Hold it right there," as the car jerked to a halt.

They pitched into the back of the vehicle and Teddy dashed to the driver's side.

*Oh, this is perfect.*

Sloan screamed, "Die, scum," yanked the gun from his belt, and pulled the trigger in apparent desperation when it failed to respond. The others pulled him inside and slammed the doors closed, and the van peeled out before the shots from the police could penetrate the metal. They had chosen their escape route wisely to include a couple of tunnels and a highway and were free and clear in no time.

Mur laughed and patted him on the back. "You're a crazy man, Ketch. I guess Teddy was right about you. Consider yourself part of the team."

The agent grinned and nodded with what he thought was the right mixture of smugness and excitement.

*Phase one complete.*

## CHAPTER NINETEEN

Diana, Rath, and Anik crossed the threshold into Kayleigh's lab, a place where the Agents of BAM Pittsburgh were rarely invited. Her space had a very different feel from the one in DC, which was a powerful testimony to the ways in which she thought and operated differently from Emerson. Two worktables were positioned in the center of the room with walking space around each. Computer terminals attached to a variety of equipment ran down the right-hand wall. Laser cutters and 3D printers stretched along the opposite one and performed their tasks with quiet whirs.

Where the tables in DC had been filled with works in progress, this entire workspace was meticulously clean. Everything was in its appointed place. There was no office, only a small desk in the back that she abandoned as she moved to greet them. A row of cabinets identical to the ones that held their operational gear a floor below stood behind her desk. The tech donned a scowl. "Welcome to my lab. Touch nothing."

Rath grinned. "*Ready Player One*. Great film." She gave him a grin and a nod, and Diana realized she'd probably need to schedule more movie time to keep up with the troll.

The blonde pushed the hair out of her face. "So, what do you want to talk about—defense or equipment? And where are the other three?"

Diana was more excited about the gear, so she decided to do the less fun part first. "Defense. Tony and Cara are out on a consult, then going after a level-two. It shouldn't be a problem." The security consulting and bounty hunting agency slowly gained traction, and Tony did a fantastic job as its visible leader. His detective skills made him good at reading people. Sloan would have been a valuable addition, too, if they didn't need to keep him off the radar. "Our Face is out doing Face things, I presume."

Kayleigh nodded. "Defense it is." She gestured toward one of the tables and retrieved a black box with a large lens on the top from a cabinet. Once she'd positioned the device on the worktable, she pressed the activation button. A holographic projection appeared in the air above it, and the tech manipulated the image with gestures.

*Damn. I really need to get some of those sensors.*

Diana laughed inwardly as she looked at her hands. *But first, I have to quit breaking my nails in fights, I suppose.*

The picture zoomed in on the parking area. "Okay, we've added a suite of detectors at the entrance to the base's level of the garage. Our cars will have a transponder inside to allow them to enter without setting off an alert. If anyone else drives in, we'll all know about it."

Anik asked, "Won't that lead to a slew of false alarms?"

Kayleigh shrugged, and the projection shifted a little in response. "Probably. But the cameras are easily checked, and any one of us can clear the signal through the AR interface."

"That's good, but what happens if we do find an enemy in the garage?" Diana pressed.

The picture zoomed to show the tunnel. "I arranged for some surplus military drones—older models—to be shipped in a while ago to play with." She wiggled her fingers to manipulate the image and another image appeared, looking like a 3D blueprint. "I stripped the weapons, mounted them on a pan-tilt head and tripod, and attached the drone's optical equipment to a motion sensing suite."

Diana put the pieces together and smiled. "You've created automated turrets."

Kayleigh nodded. "The systems will register our watches, of course, so we don't trigger them. I'll have them installed in the tunnel later today, tomorrow at the latest."

"Stun?" Anik inquired.

"The ones nearest the garage, yes. Probably four of them, based on the time available and materials at hand. The last pair will be drum-fed NATO 5.56."

The demolitions expert whistled. "Nice. We could rig claymores in the passage, too, if you wanted."

Kayleigh grinned. "We can talk later." Anik nodded and matched her smile. "Anyway, that's the tunnel. Our security that prevents those upstairs from getting down here is already strong, and nothing short of a rocket launcher will penetrate the stairwell door. The coworking spaces above...well, they are a different matter."

The schematic vanished and the image of the building rotated. "Given the need to keep up the cover business, there are people in and out at all hours. Over the next week, I'll have techs up from DC to install better sensing gear throughout. Cameras, sniffers, and whatever they have in storage. I'd also like to blow our entire existing bankroll on anti-magic emitters."

Diana shook her head in regret rather than negation. She put a whine into her words. "Do we have to?"

The tech nodded. "I think so. There's no one we suspect of being magic-reliant on the list, so it shouldn't be a big deal. We'll need to offer an explanation, so we could say that we heard the other office building was brought down by magic and corporate has overreacted. We can put something official out on the website, that sort of thing."

Anik frowned. "Won't that seem like discrimination?"

"Yes, that's the main problem. It could easily be taken that way, which would look bad for the shell company and really rotten for us if the connection to ARES goes public. Still, it's the safest route."

Diana sighed. "I have to say no to this. It's not a good look. Plus, that's not what we're about. We don't have anything against the people using magic legitimately, only those who feel the desire to screw over others with their powers."

Kayleigh expelled a breath. "God, I really hoped you'd say that. I didn't want to do it either, but someone had to make the suggestion."

*That's it. You're staying. I will find a way. That's exactly the kind of commitment I need on my team.*

*Didn't we already say that?*

*Shut up, me.*

"Well done, people. Good thinking. So, any other thoughts on the floors above?"

"More guards and better guards," Anik suggested,

Kayleigh added, "We stop using it entirely. If no one sees us up there, they won't be able to put the company together with ARES."

Diana nodded. "Those are both good ideas. Let's make them happen. We can do offsites if we need to meet people." She paused and snapped her fingers. "Anik, you're now our vehicle supervisor. Congratulations. That's a huge honor. Give those folks a call and have them do tinted windows all around. We'll try to keep a lower profile everywhere—and other options rather than governmental black, too."

"Got it, boss. Consider it done."

"I have thoughts on the cars, too," Kayleigh added. "If it's cool with you, we'll add more than transponders and tinting. I want to increase their sensor range and store a few of my toys in each."

*That sounds like fun.*

"Your wish is Anik's command, oh mighty chief technician." The demolitions expert shook his head with a laugh.

"Good." Kayleigh nodded. "I think that's all we are able to do defense-wise inside. There will be more surveillance on the outside as well. I'll send a continuous feed to DC, where one of the staff can help us keep an eye on things. The delay is minimal, and it means we don't have to vet another person up here yet." She shut the projector down and returned it to the cabinet, then closed the door carefully. "Okay, let's move on to the fun stuff."

The tech crossed to the next locker, retrieved a new version of the stun gun, and tossed it to Diana. She caught the weapon and was immediately impressed. "It's maybe half as heavy?"

"Fifty-two percent of the original weight, with a thirteen percent increase in power. It probably still won't work on Kilomea, though, unless they're small."

The troll said, "Stupid Mirennas."

Kayleigh grinned. "I took your idea and ran with it, Rath." She pointed to a switch positioned where the trigger group on their carbines were located. "Up is standard. Down is spread beam. That will make it easier to catch bouncy things and maybe even get a few at once."

Diana sighted down the barrel and lined up the targeting bump. "Damn, girl. Nice work."

She laughed. "I'm awesome. I know. It's a heavy burden, but I make it look good." She took the weapon back and stored it in the cabinet. "I don't want to take your current gear offline while I do the mods, so expect it to be a week or so before I have the replacements ready."

The next item she revealed looked a lot like a metal collar. "This is something entirely new. I thought about the comms problems you had in the museum and about our increasing need to add a technological edge to your missions and eventually made this." She turned the ring over in her hands so they could view it from all angles. The object appeared to be nothing more than a circle of metal with a slight bulge where the pieces joined.

Diana grinned. "It's pretty. I think it will go with almost everything I own. It's nice of you to be concerned about the team's fashion sense, and speaking of which…"

The blonde rolled her eyes. "No, the boots aren't ready. Relax about the footwear, woman." She continued to turn the metal circle in her hands. "This little beauty does several things. First, it pairs with the repeaters that you'll wear to increase signal output locally and in general. It feeds your earpieces and should be a better microphone than the one currently installed in them. Second, the device will send your biometric data back to me—fully encrypted, of course. Third, it interfaces with your AR glasses. But best of all, the collar has a basic AI built in, meaning you can interact by voice when needed."

Diana couldn't hide her amazement. "Holy hell. You got all of that in there?"

The tech nodded. "Yes. And it wasn't easy, let me tell you. I'll need to map each of your necks because it has to lay perfectly so all the sensors are able to do their jobs." She turned to the troll. "Except for Rath, since I have your three-foot size fully imaged. Yours will be held magnetically to break away if you grow. But please pick up the pieces if at all possible. This stuff is expensive."

They laughed, and she stored the prototype in the cabinet before turning back to them. "You can choose male or female voice for your AI and give it whatever name you like. Each collar will be backed up in an individual quarantine on a real-time basis."

Anik beat Diana to the punch. "Male. Jarvis."

"Damn. Jerk. Okay. Female, Friday."

The tech laughed. "Don't you have any original ideas, people?"

Diana put her hands on her hips. "What's yours?"

Kayleigh went from triumphant to abashed in an instant. “Male. Alfred. I get your point. Shut up.”

Rath grinned. “Female. Gwen.”

She groaned. “Another Marvel fan. Honestly, you people. Get a grip. We’re a lot closer to Batman than we are to any of the others.”

The troll shook his head. “Iron Tech.”

Kayleigh laughed and looked at Diana, who nodded and gestured for her to continue. “Rath, we’ve talked about making you part of the surveillance team for the building. What do you think?”

The troll’s voice was guarded but carried a hint of excitement. “Is good. Different. New. More learning. What is needed?”

The team had discussed how to inspire Rath, and all the answers came with risks attached. They’d agreed that he’d be most useful doing what he did best—keeping an eye on the city. Still, Diana’s tone reflected her uneasiness with the plan. “We want you to do a security sweep for us as often as it fits into your other activities. We have surveillance, but you can totally spot things the cameras and algorithms would miss.”

He cocked his head. “Here? Home? University?”

She nodded. “All of those and more. The security agency, too. Basically, learn the place to identify problems before we see them in any other way.”

“And,” Kayleigh added, “I’ll have some new gear for you to use while you do it. That should be ready in a week to ten days.”

Rath grinned. “Is good. Rath and Gwen will patrol. And sometimes Max.”

Diana nodded. "Is good."

Anik looked at them all like they were crazy, then shrugged. "Keep an eye out for stuff that needs blowing up, my friend." He raised his fist for a bump, and the troll obliged.

"Will. Boom. Big Bada Boom."

## CHAPTER TWENTY

"Damn it to hell." Diana threw up her hands in frustration as the portal she tried to create failed. Again.

Nylotte shook her head slowly. "You're close. Don't let the emotion win. While some magic is enhanced by strong passions, most is not, including portals."

She used her fingers to comb her hair out of her face. Offensive and defensive magic came easily to her, something the Drow mocked her about relentlessly.

*As motivation, no doubt.*

In any case, it was true that she was much better at throwing force around than at bending the universe to her demand to connect one place to another. Helpful internal-Diana added, *Or illusion. You're terrible at that, too.*

*Shut up, you.*

Diana expelled a breath and focused, using the silly ritual phrase Nylotte had taught her. "Betwixt and between, I will go." She marshaled her power on the statement of intent, and a wobbly oval appeared. The attempt looked like it might crumple at any moment. She froze and locked her gaze on it, then imagined energy flowing from her hands as she outlined the shape in the air. The rift solidified to reveal the upper floor of the shop in its wavering boundaries.

Nylotte reached over to the collection of objects that sat beside her cushion. While Diana had worked herself to exhaustion to summon the portal, her teacher had maintained an inscrutable expression, seemingly removed from the experience. Only her occasional comment, whether correction or encouragement, showed she was present in anything other than physical form.

*She's probably astral projecting or some other thing I'll never be good enough to do.*

The rift wavered and Diana refocused. The Drow hefted something that looked like an apple but was a beautiful glimmering purple that the earthly version of the fruit had no chance of ever achieving. She threw it underhand toward the portal.

It happened almost too fast to see. As the produce passed through the barrier, a tentacle whipped out and intercepted it, accompanied by a wicked shriek. The spell failed, and Diana stumbled back in surprise and fear.

*Those bloody damned mother-loving tentacles suck.*

For once, her inner voice stayed silent, apparently agreeing with her feelings about the disgusting appendages.

Nylotte shook her head. "You're closer but still not there."

Diana sighed, dropped onto the cushion across from her teacher, and caught another of the apple-like fruits the woman tossed to her. She took a bite and enjoyed the strange taste that was a blend between peach, plum, and apple. Most of the foods in the kemana were safe for humans, and the Drow had promised not to deliberately poison her.

*But that doesn't mean I'll leave my healing potion at home, either.*

The weight of the metal container on the back of her belt was reassuring. "Every portal risks the World in Between?"

The woman nodded and her pure white mane fell across her face. She tucked it behind a dark, pointed ear. "The key is creating barriers that prevent interference. In time, you will do that part automatically. But at first, it is a difficult challenge to overcome." The unspoken, "For you," was nonetheless clearly present.

*Yes, I know, children on Oriceran can do it, blah blah blah...*

"Try illusion again."

Diana closed her eyes and cleared her mind as best as she could. She opened them again and raised a palm. She pictured a flower on top of it, as Nylotte had suggested, then whispered the nonsense words that were supposed to bring it into existence. "What I see shall be." Nothing happened. She concentrated harder, but her focus was elusive and finally escaped entirely. She lowered her hand and shook her head.

The Drow grinned at her. "You're not used to challenges."

Diana blinked. "What? Of course I am. My life is nothing but challenges, one after the next."

The smile widened. "Ah, but there are challenges, and

then there are challenges. Things that oppose you but that you are adequate to contend with are not real challenges, only obstacles. You are so often sufficient without really trying that when you find something that requires you to reach beyond your limits, it causes your mind to shrink and hide."

"It does not."

The woman simply held her smile and raised an eyebrow.

"Okay, maybe a little. Sometimes. But hiding isn't the right word."

"Okay. Would you prefer cowering?"

"Stop. Can we move on to combat please?"

"Avoiding? Redirecting?"

"How about departing?"

Nylotte's laugh was a joyous thing, which continually came as a shock to Diana and probably always would. It was entirely contradictory to her teacher's general demeanor. "All right, we can return to your comfort zone, my student." The woman rose in a slow turn that uncrossed her legs and gestured to send the cushions spinning away. Diana settled into her preferred combat stance, with her weight pushed slightly back on a bent rear leg and her front knee pointing at her opponent. The Drow stood normally and her hands grasped her elbows lightly as she awaited Diana's readiness.

She nodded after a moment, and her teacher spoke. "Fire."

*Dammit. Is it too much to ask to start with something I'm actually good at?*

*Seems like,* the other Diana replied.

Diana focused and searched inside for the pool of power, then imagined it burning through the lines of her body, weaving through Chakras, and emerging in a wash of fury from her hands. Nothing happened. She conjured a force shield by reflex. It would have been adequate against a cone of flame or a fireball, but her teacher had lied. Time slowed briefly as her innate talent took over, but she'd spent too long in her own head for it to be of any use. The balls of ice slammed into her above and below the buckler. The impact, the temperature, and the magic encapsulated within the objects all hurt in different ways.

She shouted in anger as a red haze washed across her eyes and banished her modified vision. Without thinking, she extended her hands, and the chill that had invaded her body coalesced and traveled smoothly down her arms to emerge as a blizzard of ice shards that whirled at her teacher. The Drow generated a shield of the same element that reached from the floor to above her head in a protective oval to weather the storm. Diana slumped, suddenly exhausted, and Nylotte stepped forward to guide her down to the hastily summoned cushion that spun into place beneath her.

The world swirled in her sight, and she concentrated on not losing consciousness. A glass vial touched her lips. "Drink—quickly." She complied, and energy flowed down her throat and into her body, enough to stabilize her. Confused, she gazed into her teacher's concerned face.

"What happened?"

The Drow shook her head and lowered herself gracefully to sit on a cushion beside her. "You are full of surprises. That was something instinctive, gathering in the power that should harm you and using it as your own attack. I've never seen it before. If it weren't so unpredictable, it would be quite useful."

"Can we train it?"

*I sound like Rath.*

The thought of the troll made her lips curl upward.

"Perhaps. We can certainly try. But not today. You need to rest before exerting yourself again, or you could be damaged."

"Shouldn't the purple crystals protect from that? Isn't that the point of them?"

Nylotte shook her head. "For someone who was born and raised on Oriceran, they are an essential...well, resupply is probably the word that would best describe it for you. However, your connection is not as strong, so they do not benefit you as intensely. They help, but they do not alleviate the danger."

"That's good to know."

The Drow held a hand up, and a small lacquered box drifted from across the room to settle gently into it. She extended the item to Diana. "Open it."

"A gift? For me? You shouldn't have." She took the package with a wry grin and opened it to reveal a black leather bracelet a couple of inches wide. A design was impressed into the material, which was far less rigid than it seemed at first glance. She looked questioningly at her teacher.

"It's a charm bracelet. I've worked on creating one-time-use magical spells and thought it would be appropriate to use you to experiment on. Consider it part of your payment for my instruction."

Diana rolled her eyes. "Awesome. Really. Thanks."

The Drow raised a perfect white eyebrow. "There are two charms stitched inside. The material should protect you from being burned when they are consumed."

"Why do I worry when you say should? What do they do?"

"The first will enhance your perceptions. All five senses should be improved."

"There's that word again."

Nylotte cackled. "Nervous, protege?"

"Not a bit," she lied. "What's the other one?"

"Basically, the opposite of the first. It should make you harder to detect by diminishing others' senses when they are near you."

She shrugged and put the item on, then used her teeth to hold the strap while she locked the buckle in place. She looked up to find her teacher staring at her with an infuriatingly amused smile on her face. "What?"

"You don't like asking for help, do you?"

"Do you?"

"Fair point."

Diana admired the bracelet. "It looks good. Thank you. Even if I am your guinea pig." She met Nylotte's eyes. "I have a question, though." The woman gestured for her to continue. "Tell me what you know about artifacts."

"That's more a command than a question, is it not?"

"Let's not get bogged down in semantics. Spill."

The Drow showed her teeth in a mocking grin, then turned serious. "Beings have created repositories for magic since the earliest days. Some are more powerful, some less.

It varies with the process and with the skills and potential of the one who crafts them."

"The most powerful ones?"

A look of distaste swept across her teacher's face before it vanished as if it had never existed at all. "Rhazdon's artifacts hold the lives—or spirits, or powers, or remnants, or whatever you prefer to call them—of living beings. They are considered superior to all others."

"People actually had such loyalty to her that they would sacrifice themselves to become part of her artifacts?"

The Drow's voice was flat. "No."

"Oh." Diana's brain took a moment to catch up. "They didn't volunteer?" Her teacher shook her head. "That's…terrible."

"It is a violation of the most fundamental kind."

"That explains why the Remembrance is so determined to collect them. The power they hold, that is."

Nylotte nodded. "They are powerful individually, and more so once collected."

The idea sent a chill through Diana. "You mean they… uh, reinforce one another?"

"Not as such. But multiple beings with such power make life far more difficult for those who oppose them. More tentacles and such."

The chill became almost icy.

*You did that on purpose, elf-wench.*

"Well, that's a bonus." She noticed her teacher's odd expression. "What?"

"I've heard a rumor."

"Do you care to share it?"

"There is a set of artifacts crafted to work in cooperation with one another somehow that were fashioned into armor for use in Rhazdon's first rebellion."

"Okay." Diana did not like the turn this conversation had taken.

The Drow shrugged. "After a very long time of hearing nothing about it, in the last weeks, it has been mentioned in my presence more than once. It may merely be a coincidence."

"There are no coincidences. Bloody hell. How bad is this for us?"

Nylotte stared directly into her eyes, and Diana was shaken to see the depth of the naked concern she showed. "Quite bad, indeed."

## CHAPTER TWENTY-ONE

Sloan hadn't been in the dive bar this early in the day before. It was not the sort of place one actually wanted to see in bright light. He closed the door carefully behind him to shut out the illumination that revealed the airborne dust and any number of other things he didn't really want to think closely about.

Teddy sat at the bar, sipping from a tall glass containing either tomato juice or a Bloody Mary. Sloan put his money on the latter. He looked very much the worse for wear, which made sense, given the celebratory mood that had filled the gang since their successful heist several nights before.

He turned his grey beard to Sloan and said, "Hey, Ketch. 'Sup?"

The agent clapped him on the shoulder as he took the tall stool beside him. "Living. Loving. Causing trouble. The usual. You?"

Teddy raised his red drink in a toast. "Holding down

the fort and getting my energy back." Sloan noticed belatedly that there was no one behind the bar.

"You're working here?"

The man waggled a hand in the air. "Not really. More filling in while Geetch is out buying supplies. It's not like anyone comes in this early."

Sloan made a show of looking around. "Yeah, and you can see why. When's the last time they deep-cleaned in here?"

The older man gave a scratchy laugh. "World War Two, probably. But the booze is good and cheap, and no one bothers us."

"Y'all should get a clubhouse. A base of operations."

Teddy shrugged. "Here works. For now, anyway. Maybe soon, things will change a little."

"How so?"

He took a long swig of his drink and swiveled on the stool to face Sloan. "We have something bigger than usual on the way. Mur is setting it up with some friends of his. It's gonna be a good payday."

Sloan grinned. "Another break-in? That was smooth as silk the other night."

"Kind of. He'll be here in a few to explain it, along with the rest of the boys."

"Did I screw the time up?"

"No. I wanted you here a little early so we could have a word." He seemed uncomfortable, and a flash told Sloan he had some uncertainty about something. He took a guess at what it might be.

"Is this about the gun? It's okay that it misfired. No harm, no foul."

*That should make him think I don't suspect a thing.*

Teddy gave him a half smile. "Good. I felt bad about giving you a piece that didn't work."

"It's not like you had a way of knowing. Sometimes stuff goes wrong."

"True enough." Any further words were rendered inaudible by the sound of the front door banging open, and the offensive-lineman-sized leader of the group pushed through. Teddy stood. "Hiya, Mur. Drink?"

The man shook his head. "No time. Places to be. Let's go back."

Teddy moved past the newcomers and locked the door. Sloan trailed him as he followed the others into the rear of the bar, where they gathered again around the card table. This time, he was the one left without a chair, which suited him fine. The other two men had been on the heist with them, but Sloan hadn't been introduced. They stared at him with a mixture of distrust and a distinct lack of welcome.

"We have a gig working for some friends of mine." There were supportive nods, the kind that followers gave when sucking up to a leader who calculated loyalty minute by minute.

Sloan added his own slight nod but wasn't about to play the pandering wannabe. He sensed the man's respect wouldn't be won by over-subordination. "It's nice to have friends, like you said."

Teddy laughed uncomfortably, and his voice cracked from the alcohol he'd already consumed. Mur looked at Sloan but didn't reply. For his part, the agent maintained eye contact and gave them what he thought of as his blank face. Finally, the leader broke the silence. "It is, indeed, Ketch." He turned to the group. "We'll hit the University. They have a special collection on exhibit in the Library—some old books from this world and the other one. It should be a score that gets us some good cash."

Sloan frowned.

*Odd.*

"What do your friends need a bunch of books for?" He injected a note of bewilderment into his tone.

Mur frowned at him and leaned back to stare. "I'm not sure why you care, new guy, but the answer is I don't know. And I don't want to know, either. They're the kind of friends that when they ask you to do a thing, you do it."

He held up a hand in apology. "I'm not criticizing, only curious. Is there anything else in there we can grab while we're at it? Do they mind a little freelancing?"

The leader's lips spread in a cautious smile. "Now that's the first useful question you've asked. It seems like you're the right person to find out. Does that sound good?"

Sloan nodded. "I know some people. Not friends, not really, but also not above trading inside information for cash. I'll check in with them."

Mur nodded. "We'll do the heist one night next week. Everything has to run like clockwork. We'll go in when the library closes, right after midnight. The books will be in the secure exhibit on the fifth floor. I already have a contact to let us in." He snapped his fingers and turned to Teddy. "We gonna need stun guns for this one. We'll blast him so there's no suspicion afterward, and any other resistance will be only students and rent-a-cops. There's no reason to bring heavy hardware." Unsaid was the fact that if they were arrested, they'd get a lighter sentence if they carried only non-lethal weapons.

*Somehow, I doubt Mur will go in unstrapped, though.*

The meeting adjourned and the others took their leave. Sloan was left with Teddy and the man still seemed uncomfortable. As he had on many occasions before, the agent wished he could summon his magic at will.

*Heh. Maybe the scary elf everyone talks about can train me next.*

But his mundane senses screamed that something was up, and his mantra in situations like that was to get simple, get clear, and get clean. He raised a fist for a bump, and Teddy met it with relief in his eyes. "Text when you need me, bruh. Y'all are my main job right now, and I'm up for whatever. I'll go see what I can find out about the library."

He nodded and unlocked the front door to let Sloan out into the sun. Outside, he squinted at it and looked around as if deciding what to do next. Down the hill and to the right, the road led to a string of more dive bars and a strip club that touted itself as the best place to watch sports in town.

*Sports, right. Sure.*

To the left, the long walk through the strip district would return him to the city proper. His dingy hotel stood about halfway between here and there, but he wasn't sure it would be smart to go there immediately.

He ambled slowly down the hill, slipped on his sunglasses, inserted his earbuds, and looked at his phone. A few swipes activated the AR functions, and he left the camera on to feed into the eyewear's display. He swung his arms as he walked to make sure the lens had a look in all directions and finally spotted the tail. The two other men from the bar took turns to stay close while one paralleled him a block away on either side.

*They're trying hard not to spook me. And they're not terrible at tracking, either. A point to them.*

He had several options available. A simple set of counter-surveillance moves would lose them, but it risked them realizing that he'd made them.

*So, that's out.*

He could pretend to notice them by chance and confront them about following him. That might increase his standing with them, and maybe Mur and Teddy, but it could also have the opposite result and increase their suspicions. He certainly wouldn't let them trail him to the hotel. His mind sifted through other possibilities, but they were all risky, and he didn't want to jeopardize his connection to the gang.

Only one option remained. He boarded the next bus and dropped his fare in the till before he shuffled to a seat at the back. While he bounced his head in time to the music playing in his ears, he typed a text to the operations number, which would be monitored by whoever was in the base at the moment.

**Heading to someplace called Homestead Waterfront. Bus 5349. Need a tail check.**

The encrypted message sent and vanished seconds later, while all record of it was wiped from his device.

The response was immediate.

**Ops. K.**

*So, Kayleigh.*

**Check inbound.**

A dozen minutes passed before he received a one-word follow-up.

**Clean.**

She must have detailed a drone or two to follow him and make sure his watchers had been left behind.

He typed again.

**Cool. Ride?**

Her answer was brief and brutal.

**Bus trip back is as scenic. Enjoy.**

He shook his head. The tech was a tough cookie, but he'd win her over eventually. So far, she'd proven immune to his charms, but then again, he hadn't really tried yet.

*You know, what I truly need to make this cover persona work is a girlfriend. I wonder how easily we could disguise her.*

He spent the rest of the trip considering options to improve Tommy Ketchum's viability, only a few of which involved the hyper-intelligent blonde technician. But the ones that did were his favorites.

# CHAPTER TWENTY-TWO

Vincente's office was as dark as he could make it. The doors were closed and the lights turned off. Blinds covered the windows he so often paced in front of to shut out the rest of the warehouse. The only illumination came from the statuette before him via a soft glow that never left the crystal at the top.

His coin felt heavy where it burned against his chest, signaling his superior's desire for communication. The wizard sighed, withdrew the object from the small pocket inside his shirt, and slotted it into place at the base of the sculpture. The device performed its magic, and a three-dimensional image of Dreven appeared and hovered above the crystal.

"Master." The artifact within him seemed to twist, disliking any act of subordination. Whispers from the entity—it seemed appropriate to call it that—had assaulted his mind at random times. It demanded that he seize power and spun plans to ascend in the ranks. It didn't have the best understanding of the situation at hand, but it was very committed to the idea of becoming the most powerful being around.

*In time. For now, we must serve.*

The image nodded. "Vincente. What is the status of your team?"

*Lousy, thanks for asking. How's yours?*

He cleared his throat. "As expected, Sarah has…recovered from her experience in the World in Between. The humans still lack a leader with Marcus locked in the human prison." He schooled his voice to contain the hope he felt. "Will we attack the installation to rescue our people in the near future, Master?"

Dreven nodded. "Soon, but not yet. We have another objective in the interim."

"And my people will be a part of securing this objective?"

"Among many others across many operations, yes. You will be my personal representatives in this undertaking, and as you are in charge of the primary assignment, failure would be…unacceptable, to say the least." The venom contained in the threat was unmistakable. His artifact bristled, and Vincente's lips twitched. He covered it with a sneer.

"If there is a disappointment of any kind, Master, it will not come from us."

The virtual wizard nodded. "Excellent. In preparation for the event, you are to bestow an artifact upon your subordinate."

He couldn't contain the grimace. "Do you think that's wise, Master?"

"Would I instruct you to do it if I did not?"

Vincente sighed. "Of course not. I will do as you say."

Dreven gave him a knowing smile. "There are reasons for everything, my trusted lieutenant. Have faith." For a moment, warmth crept into his voice. It vanished as quickly to be usurped by aloof certainty. "The event occurs in less than a week and requires a full commitment from you and all your people."

"You have it, of course, Master."

"Once there are details to share, they will be communicated to you. The location is still uncertain, and thus the timing is in flux. Events shall move quickly once these things are known. You must be ready at a moment's notice."

"We will be."

His superior nodded. "I know that you will. Now, empower your second in command and prepare for what is to come."

"Yes, Master."

The connection dropped as the image turned to vapor and spiraled away. Vincente withdrew the coin and returned it to the inner pocket, then buttoned his black shirt and smoothed his black tie into place. He had a flash of self-analysis accompanied by a mocking laugh.

*Once, there was color in my life, but neither power nor responsibility. Now, I possess those things but have abandoned visual variety for trustworthy darkness.*

He laughed at himself again.

*Subtle metaphor, man. Real deep.*

He stood, walked to the safe, and spun the lock open on the first try. He had changed the combination the day before. Concerns over security even there in his stronghold had grown with the passage of time. Marcus's absence was a persistent hindrance that required him to interact with the man's followers far more than he preferred to. Still, every soldier was necessary, now more than ever. He merely wished they could free their imprisoned people, one and all. It irked him that they were so physically near, yet he could do nothing for them. There was an edge of loyalty to the feeling but statistics won over. This was a numbers game, after all. Marcus was worth any five of his disciples, and the gang was ultimately weaker without him.

He opened the door to call for Sarah, but she was already standing on the landing outside. He blinked in surprise but managed not to flinch. The paleness that had marked her return into the world had not changed. Her eyes were still a vivid blue and looked shocking in the colorlessness that surrounded them. Three scars ran diagonally across each cheek, white on white. A healing potion had closed the wounds but failed to remove the reminders. They were lightly touched with scarlet makeup, and a faint red on her lips captured the same hue. He'd begun to think of the whole look as her war paint.

Before the incident, she had possessed a wardrobe of varying colors and styles. Now, she wore only tight black dresses with flowing skirts that reached to her ankles and black boots beneath. Long sleeves covered her arms and looped around her thumbs to keep the fabric taut. She had never been fleshy but had become almost cadaverously thin. Her sharp cheekbones and spindly fingers caused something inside him to recoil defensively. Her grim and knowing smile made it that much worse.

"Sarah. Do come in."

She swept past him and sat upright in the chair in front of his desk. She stared hungrily at the fabric-wrapped object that rested upon it. A change thrummed in the air as the two came together, including the sensation of a palpable increase in danger. Vincente swallowed hard against the desire to give in to the internal voices that told him unequivocally not to do this thing. He crossed deliberately behind the desk and sat in his chair to lean forward with his elbows on the flat surface.

"My superiors agreed to my request to grant you an artifact."

*That's mostly true, I suppose.*

He had been the one to mention the idea long before. Had it been solely his decision, though, recent events might have swayed him to delay the gift indefinitely. "This is a great honor for you but comes with a commensurate burden."

Sarah nodded. "I understand. I will use this power—and all my power—in the service of the goals of the Remembrance."

He wasn't fooled by her phrasing.

*Not for me, and not for those above, but for the "goals" as you perceive them. Truth, but not truth, all at once.*

It didn't matter. No one expected her to act differently, and the artifacts demanded their own loyalty, even before the Remembrance added the not-so-subtle magics to keep their followers in line.

He pushed the fabric bundle across to her without a word. Her hand trembled as she unwrapped the heavy scarlet cover fold by fold. Her breath came faster with each layer removed. She gasped when the full relic was revealed.

A spiral snake coiled in upon itself, seemingly asleep. Its scales were jeweled, the body beneath a deep green that made him think of poison. Unlike his own artifact, which had been neutral or even positive toward him before the bonding, this one was unsettling.

*Maybe that's how you feel about all other artifacts once you have one. Who the hell knows? It fits her, though.*

She stared at the item before her without blinking, like she somehow communed with it. She reached out tentatively, still shaking, and touched her finger to the mouth of the serpent. The artifact moved as if it had been alive the whole time and merely bided its time. It flowed over her hand to twine around her arm under her sleeve. The traveling bulge was disconcerting. More uncomfortable was the witch's moan as it climbed and the look of ecstasy the bonding inspired on her pale features. Her expression transformed suddenly to reflect shock and brutal pain, but it subsided in an instant as the artifact sank into her flesh and the bulge vanished.

Her head lolled back in the chair, and her exposed neck caused his artifact to twist again and whisper in his mind.

*Kill her. Do it now.*

He pushed the impulse aside.

The witch soon recovered her senses and raised her head with a soft smile as she stretched her arms high. "The power…" She breathed a slow, heady breath. "It's delicious."

Vincente nodded. "Remember the responsibility that accompanies it, Sarah."

Her grin slowly stretched wider. "The artifact has told me of the attempts to layer persuasion and obedience upon its magic. Perhaps you were aware of this?" He stilled his expression, and she waved airily. "No matter. Rest assured that I possess the strength to resist them. Before my sojourn in the World in Between, I might have been swayed. Now, it is but a minor whisper, easily ignored."

She stood and suddenly leaned toward him. He slid his chair back several inches but otherwise, did not react. She grinned, and the expression was entirely wrong on her gaunt and scarred face. "We will achieve our goals. Have no doubt. I look forward to our next task."

She walked from the room with a confidence she had lacked when she entered and closed the door lightly behind her. He crossed and clicked the lock, then cast a barrier to secure it and leaned against the frame.

*Somehow, when she says, "our goals," I don't think she's referring to the operation Dreven has tasked us with.*

He sighed.

*As if things weren't messed up enough already.*

# CHAPTER TWENTY-THREE

Things had been quiet enough that the team was well-rested, for once. They had deliberately chosen not to take any bounty gigs while they got their figurative feet back under them. However, it was time for more action lest they lose their edge. Diana had pushed the randomize button on the training ground in the rear of the Two Worlds Security office the night before and looked forward to practicing with her team.

She arrived before the others and put the coffee on, then went into the back. The computer system and autonomous forklifts had done their work, and there was now a trio of hallways rather than the single one that had been there when she left. It would be the first time using the space for Kayleigh, Sloan, and Anik, and she was excited to see what they'd bring to the table. Those three would play the opposing force for the initial round, and Kayleigh had already promised unexpected surprises. After the laser grenade that Bryant had snuck in on a previous run, she had no doubt the tech had something evil up her sleeve.

The others arrived shortly after—Kayleigh and Cara together, and the men singly. The early arrivals traded jokes while they waited for the full complement to arrive. Anik was the last one in, still several minutes ahead of the announced meeting time. Each took a long look at the entrances to the course upon entering, no doubt seeking any advantage, however small, exactly as she had. Sadly, the hallways turned almost immediately and so preserved their secrets.

They geared up quickly, strapped the detectors on, and ensured that their batteries were properly charged. Taunts were exchanged, and the trio of defenders melted away into the labyrinth, one departing down each hallway. Diana watched until they made the turns that hid them from view, then drew her team together with a wave. "I have only two things to say before we go in. First, keep your eyes peeled. Kayleigh brings a new dimension to the game. Second, since we're likely to face challenges that could cost us a victory, Tony's lead on the initial run. I certainly don't want the blame if we lose."

Cara laughed and he shook his head. The detective clapped his hands briskly. "All right, then. It's up to me to maintain the honor of BAM Pittsburgh against these heathen rebels." He checked his watch. "Another three minutes before we can go in. Any useful ideas, troops?"

Diana rolled her eyes. "Shoot them before they shoot us."

"Look out for tripwires," Cara countered.

She raised an eyebrow. "Try not to break any ribs."

The other woman laughed. "Avoid patches of ice."

Tony intervened. "Okay, people, behave. Honestly, I don't know why a leader of my vision and talent would have hired either of you." They chuckled. "But we'll have to make do. Diana, you're lead. Cara, middle. I'll bring up the rear. At any intersections, it's straight, left, right. The same rules apply for entering a room."

It was a standard deployment, one that played to their strengths. Cara was every bit as good at taking point as she was, but Diana's ability to detect magical threats made her the better choice. Tony had the least combat experience among them, so it was logical for him to trail the others. He finished the impromptu briefing by asking, "Questions?"

Cara raised her hand. He groaned. "Yes, you, the annoying one in the front row."

"Mister Ryan, sir, what if we encounter scary strangers along the way?"

Tony grinned. "Like the boss said, shoot them before they shoot you."

The head-start time expired, and they lined up at the right entrance farthest from where Kayleigh had disappeared into the stacked crates. Sloan and Anik were also unknown quantities, but the tech was Diana's biggest concern. The way her eyes had lit up when she learned she'd train with them was downright alarming, in retrospect.

*She definitely has some clever tricks waiting for us.*

Diana crept forward and scanned in a zig-zag pattern from floor to ceiling and back again. She paused at every corner as they moved deeper. After several turns, a short hallway expanded into a room beyond. No egress was visible from where she stopped the team. "What do you think, Tony?"

"Standard entrance. Since we can't see another exit, we'll commit to clearing the room before we move on."

"Affirmative. On zero." She tapped her glasses to initiate a ten-second countdown. They weren't using any AR functionality other than the timer. Diana worried about becoming overdependent on any tech and tried to balance things whenever it was practical to do so. The lack of them almost proved to be the team's undoing.

She had barely shifted her weight to break into a run when a strange glint made her stumble and hiss, "Hold." Instinctively, she fell to one knee to kill her momentum. She'd already scanned the doorway for traps and found it clear, but her lean forward had given her the necessary angle to see the tiny device. Most laser tripwires would have been set into the walls of the hallway. These were cleverly positioned inside the room and had a ninety-degree bend to send the beam across the entrance.

*Oh, clever girl. Wench.*

Diana searched carefully around the opening and discovered another pair that sliced through the space at a diagonal. She shook her head.

"Kayleigh's damn good, y'all. We have a small area to crawl through here." She pointed at the lower left corner. "We'll be seriously exposed when we do it. It doesn't seem like our normal beam blockers will reach far enough to beat these things, so we don't have much choice."

Tony laughed. "We could go for coffee. They'll come out eventually, right?"

"We could send Tony in first," Cara suggested. "Use him as a shield."

"I think we'll stick with crawling through. Those were good ideas, though, really." Diana lowered herself onto her stomach and crawled forward. She risked a look into the room and found it both small and empty. "No enemies visible. I'm going in." She wriggled through the opening and grunted as she rolled away. Immediately, she scrambled to her feet and traversed her rifle in a circle in case any unexpected opponents appeared. None did. "Come on in."

Cara was next while Diana watched the room's forward exit, which was offset from their entrance point by several crate-widths. Tony joined them last. His bigger frame presented a challenge, but he contorted himself surprisingly well and made it through. He was breathing hard when he stood. "Tricky."

Diana looked up and saw the laser grenade fastened above the doorway with a wireless receiver attached to accept a signal from the tripwires and shook her head. "She's good at everything she does, apparently."

Cara grinned cheekily. "Thanks. That means a lot coming from you." Her boss rolled her eyes and she chuckled. "Oh—you didn't mean me? I'm wounded."

Diana was already looking down the exit hall but spared a moment to raise a finger at her second in command. "There's a dogleg ahead. It could be a wonderful place for an ambush. Grenades would be useful."

Tony tutted and shook his head with a smirk. "You can't blow every problem up, boss."

"Name one that you can't."

He didn't reply, and she paced carefully down the passage. When she reached the dogleg, she pushed out with her rifle ready. Again, no one laid in wait. She paused to let the adrenaline settle before she continued. After another set of turns, the hall took on a configuration she hadn't seen before that was half as high as usual.

"This is ugly, y'all." The others advanced into the corridor behind her and groaned in agreement.

Tony urged her on. "You're the shortest, so this is all you."

"You can bite my—" She left the line unfinished as she contemplated the chokepoint and smiled when she remembered her first exercise in the field. It had been paintballs back then. This was the perfect place for another laser grenade.

*Good thinking, people.*

However, it was possible that they hadn't considered all the ramifications of that choice, and she was ready to help them do so. She turned to Cara and handed off her rifle. "Hold this for me."

The other woman grinned. "My pleasure."

Diana crawled into the low space. The passage was five crates long—or about ten feet—before it appeared to return to normal height. She was halfway in when the anticipated projectile bounced into her line of sight from the corner ahead and skipped along the floor toward her. Her right hand happened to be the one in front, so she raised it and flicked her fingers to boomerang the device back. It reversed course and banked off the wall in the direction from which it had come. It seemed her grenade-billiards skills proved adequate to the occasion. The grenade detonated with an odd electronic shriek, followed by the buzz of a fatal hit and a deep, "Dammit," yelled from down the hall. Diana grinned and continued her advance, then stood and stuck her head around the corner for a quick look.

Anik sat on the floor with a stormy scowl on his face. All his sensors lit up to show that he was well and truly "dead." He looked at her smile and shook his head. "Not cool, boss."

She shrugged and tried to make her tone instructive rather than of celebratory. "It's a brave new world, Anik. You gotta keep magic in mind." He sighed and nodded.

Cara joined them and shot the downed man with her laser rifle. He gazed at her with a question on his face. "You could have been faking," she said cheerfully. "It's always best to be sure."

Tony fired immediately, and when they turned to stare at him, said, "What? She's right."

The team reassembled and moved forward. They advanced through the labyrinth—which was far more twisted than previous designs had been—and finally reached a place where the hallway forked. Diana looked cautiously down each path, but neither seemed immediately preferable. She growled softly and selected the one on the left. Her mental prediction had been that the two courses would intersect again, but an opening appeared ahead instead. The doorway was half-blocked by a lowered crate.

*Damn, this is a wicked map.*

"So, this is ugly, part two."

The others stepped up behind her and agreed. Tony quipped "Very dangerous. You go first."

"Thanks bunches, tough guy." Diana decided that boldness would be her best option and hurtled forward to slide at the last instant to pass under the barrier and careen into the chamber. She pushed onto her feet and dodged to the side the instant she was past the obstacle. Her eyes scanned the room and found it mostly empty—except for a bulwark in the corner made of stacked crates, a rifle barrel that protruded over it, and an odd glitter on the ceiling. The barrel of the weapon aimed at a shiny object mounted above, and it took her a moment to realize it was a prism.

There was no time to react as the enemy fired and the laser beam refracted in all directions. Diana's arm was hit first and then her leg as she scrambled away. The next shot led to a kill, and she groaned. A ruckus ensued from the hallway as more fire was exchanged, rapidly followed by the sound of another pair of deaths. Cara slipped under the obstruction with her weapon already searching for a target but met the same fate as Diana.

Kayleigh emerged from her small fortress, her grin wide and triumphant. She peered smugly at the fallen agents. "What's it like being dead?"

Cara rolled onto her back and stared at her foe. "Boss, I think we need a set of shock gear for this one."

The tech looked confused, and Diana laughed. "For sure. Snipers and techs receive the special treatment from here on out."

Tony called from the hallway, "I'm dead again. Does anyone care?"

Diana rose with a laugh. "Maybe you should be more

careful, Tony. You seem to get killed a lot." She turned to Kayleigh with a grin of her own. "The best part about training? There's always a round two where you seek revenge on those who have wronged you." She flicked the fingers of her left hand, and a small telekinetic yank tweaked Kayleigh's ponytail. The tech's eyes widened, and Diana laughed again. "You're not the only one with tricks."

*My pretty, this little party's only beginning.*

# CHAPTER TWENTY-FOUR

The summons to meet at the bar had been unexpected. It wasn't one of the normal nights for the group to get together as far as Sloan knew. Kayleigh had marked the place as a location of interest in the system, so whenever GPS showed a drone or police car camera nearby, the computers recorded the feeds and flagged them for her attention. She hadn't identified anything out of the ordinary, either.

The normal late-afternoon crowd filled the seats—old folks who'd come to the tavern for years and newcomers from the gentrified neighborhoods that surrounded it looking for something different.

*Well, this place is certainly that.*

He waved at the bartender and strode to the back, where Mur and Teddy awaited him in the office. There were no others present.

*Uh oh. What's up with that?*

Teddy flashed him a smile, and Mur waved his paw of a

hand at a chair beside him. Sloan sat and noticed a sheen of sweat on the bald man's head.

*He's nervous about something. What?*

His talent gave him no insight, as usual. It never seemed to work when he wanted it to. Sloan looked at Teddy, but the other man avoided eye contact. Mur cleared his throat. "This job we're doing at the library… It turns out that for you, it might be the proverbial golden egg."

Sloan performed the mental shift fully into his cover persona and forced an expression of excitement onto his face. "That's awesome, Mur. Thanks for thinking of me."

Teddy laughed nervously, and Mur glared at him until he subsided. The big man was all in black today in a button-down over work pants of some kind. It was a more formal look for him compared to the jeans and garish shirts he normally wore.

*It must be something important.*

He returned his gaze to Sloan's. "The thing is, the folks we're working with asked about you personally."

He frowned. "Why? Who are they? How do they know me?"

Mur turned his hands over, the palms up on the table. "Exactly my question when I heard. It turns out that your effort to take out the police that first night impressed one of the boys enough that he mentioned it to the wrong ears. PD is interested in you, and this group is interested in the PD."

Sloan blinked.

*It's probably nonsense. He's trying to make me nervous. But it is possible if one of them felt jealous or slighted by my addition to the gang. Either way, it means trouble.*

He shook his head. "I guess I need to be more careful."

The big man shrugged. "What's done is done. The important part is that someone above has taken an interest. That means you could help the rest of us or hurt the rest of us. I wanted to be sure you remembered that Teddy and I made this introduction possible for you." Mur's words sounded oddly formal.

"No worries, there, guys. I'm a team player all the way. You gave me a chance, and I'm loyal."

They both smiled. Teddy said, "Right answer. I knew we could count on you."

Mur looked less convinced but his expression remained stoically unperturbed.

*He's waiting to see what happens before committing either way. That's a survivor move.*

"Let's hit the road."

They piled into a rusted pickup. Teddy slid into the half-sized back seat, Mur revved the engine, and they lurched into traffic. The ride needed new shocks, at least, and fresh brakes, judging by the near-misses at every stoplight. They rode through several neighborhoods before turning into an otherwise unremarkable strip mall. Mur led them into a small antique store on the end. A senior citizen with a long mane of straight gray hair sat in a tall chair behind the counter. She waved at them, and Mur reached across to take her hand with a warm smile. His gentle charm was completely unexpected. "Moira, always lovely to see you."

Her answer was colored by a thick accent that sounded like Welsh to his ears, but he wouldn't have bet a lot of money on that guess. "Murray. Causing trouble, are you?"

He laughed. "No more than usual, my dear. Have you heard anything I should know?"

She shook her head and smiled. "Only good things, love. Karl is back there waiting for you."

Mur frowned, and Sloan had the sense that the woman had shared more than a name. The bald man lifted her hand and kissed the back of it. "Be well, sweetheart." He turned to them and said, "Game faces," under his breath, then led them to the closed door at the rear of the store.

It opened onto a much wider storage area that stretched across the rear of all the stores in the small shopping center. Bundles of materials and stacks of boxes were arranged seemingly at random throughout the space. Sloan fought to keep his expression mostly neutral as his gaze identified crates of military grade weaponry among them. Several tough-looking men with rifles lingered near the garage door that led from the side wall. Another stood beside a tall man in a leather jacket and jeans. Based on the body language in the room, he was the person in charge, despite his biker-like attire.

*Or maybe because of it.*

Mur strode to him and gripped his hand, then leaned in for a chest bump. Teddy remained awkwardly at Sloan's side. For his part, the ARES Face tried to appear unthreatening and unthreatened in equal measure. The bald man waved him forward, and Sloan approached slowly. The boss stood over six feet tall and wore steel-toed work boots. His t-shirt hugged him tightly to reveal the muscles that lay underneath. A neatly trimmed dark-brown beard and mustache both matched his shortish hair. His face could best be described as unremarkable, which was perfect for one who wished to remain anonymous. A few simple earrings were his only visible jewelry. He extended a hand. "You must be Ketch. I've heard about you."

Sloan shrugged as he shook hands. "I am. I hope it's all good."

He didn't give an indication either way. "I'm Karl. Let's go into the office and talk." The room he led them to was small but well-kept, with binders filling a bookshelf next to the desk and a large safe in the corner. The man sat behind the desk, and Mur took the chair furthest to the left across from him. Sloan settled into the other, and Teddy stood near the door. The sensation of having someone standing at his six was distinctly unsettling.

Karl scratched at his beard. "So, one person tells me you're reliable, tough, and efficient. From another, I hear that you're a loose cannon who shoots at cops when it's not necessary. We have a job coming up, as you know, and I need to resolve this contradiction."

*Huh. He's smarter than he tries to appear.*

Sloan raised an eyebrow. "I can't be both?"

The man shook his head with a small smile. "In my experience, no. One is dependable. The other is not. It's a yes-no question."

"I'll go with reliable, tough, and efficient. The shots were to get their heads down, not to hit them. The gun was aimed high."

"Why shoot at all, then?"

He shrugged. "I'm not immune to the excitement of the moment. I was pumped from a great heist. It seemed like the right thing to do."

The man stared at him for longer than was comfortable, then shifted his gaze to Mur. “Do you buy it?”

He nodded. “I think he’s good.”

Karl swiveled to face him and resumed his stare. Sloan’s power finally decided to show itself in a flash that allowed him to hear the man’s thoughts.

*“Things are unsettled. I can’t afford to make a mistake. This is a big one.”*

The agent broke the silence. “Whatever the deal, I’m in. If you need me to walk, I understand. I don’t want to, but if that’s what's best, consider me gone. No harm, no foul.”

Karl nodded his understanding. “Okay. You’re in. Mur said he already explained the objective to you. What he didn’t say is that it’s part of a bigger operation, so you can’t screw it up. My reputation depends on it. I’ll take care of a different part. A single failure and the whole house of cards falls. And you do not want to be the one responsible, get me?”

Sloan nodded as Mur interjected, “Ketch is working his contacts to see if there’s anything else we need to know about the space.”

Karl looked at him expectantly and he shrugged. “Nothing different than what we already have, so far.”

The man stood. “Okay. If you do hear something, send it up through the channels. Otherwise, keep your head down and be ready. It's possible the timetable will change. If it does, we’ll have to improvise.”

They were ushered out by one of the guards. Sloan’s mind raced as he tried to put the pieces together. *This is too big to be anything other than the Remembrance. But what the hell are they up to?*

---

"What is she up to?" Max didn't answer, and Rath scowled as they slunk along behind the professor. She strode through the alleys again as she had each day since the first time they'd observed her. The troll felt an obligation to back her up, even though she could probably handle anything she was likely to encounter.

"Patrol, maybe?" Again, the Borzoi failed to weigh in. Rath drummed his fingers on the metal ring he held as they watched her turn down the street at the opposite end of the darkened path. "Follow, Max." They caught up to her several turns later. Today's route was unique, and the walk occurred closer to evening than usual.

*She's probably going to dinner or something like we should be.*

He'd left a note for Diana so she wouldn't worry. She had been both more and less protective lately, depending on the day. The new job was a big burden to all of them.

*But a good one. A necessary one.*

Which made his urge to shadow Professor Charlotte Stanley around town all the more unusual. Still, something hovered at the edge of his mind. Maybe it was instinct. Maybe there were some clues he hadn't decoded yet. Regardless, something demanded he follow this course.

Eventually, they arrived at a grand-looking old home on a beautiful street. He knew it wasn't hers. That was several blocks closer to the University. Rath watched as she marched up the stairs with purpose, tapped her wand on the door, then opened it and entered. He guided Max closer and dismounted one house away. "Stay, Max.

Listen." He rushed through the grass—which had recently been mowed, fortunately for him. The journey was simple, and his target remained in sight. He jogged around the perimeter of the house until he found a cable that came out of the ground and ran up to what was probably an attic and passed reasonably close to a first-floor window.

The troll vaulted and caught hold of it, then shimmied up the line hand-over-hand. When he reached the right height, he leapt toward the windowsill, caught it with his fingertips, and pulled himself up with a grunt. He laid on the surface and panted. When he'd caught his breath, he rolled and raised himself carefully to peer over the bottom part of the frame. Inside, three people sat at a small round table with Professor Stanley. Cups of tea steamed near each of their hands, and a teapot rested in the center. He assumed it might be a gathering of professors or a card game. They spoke animatedly, with gestures to illustrate the stories they told. He put his ear to the glass but couldn't make the words out.

He had to know.

A glance upward revealed a smaller window high above that someone had left cracked, perhaps to allow air flow. The distance was a little farther than he found comfortable but seemed doable. And if something went wrong...well, maybe he could grow fast enough that the fall wouldn't hurt so much. Hopefully.

He bounded to the cable and scaled higher until the small windowsill was closer to his level and he made the jump easily from one to the other. Rath looked down and felt a moment of vertigo but still enjoyed the sight of the high tree branches and the rooftops of the nearby houses.

The troll couldn't remember ever having been this high up before. The urge to sit and take it all in was tempting, but he had a mission. He turned, sneaked through the gap, and dropped onto a fuzzy bathroom carpet.

His feet were almost silent as he ran across the light-brown hardwood floors toward the staircase. He crept down the stairs far enough to be able to peer over the side and see the people at the table. Professor Stanley was speaking.

"And then these idiots tried to attack me in an alley. Honestly, they were far more stupid than dangerous." The others laughed. One of them, a man who looked to be the oldest with his long beard, added his own tale. "On the subway this morning, some guy was bothering a woman who was traveling by herself. The way she looked away made it obvious she didn't want to deal with him, but he blocked her access to the aisle. When we went into a tunnel, right before the inside lights kicked on, I put a sleep spell on him."

The others laughed and congratulated him on the clever action. Rath couldn't help smiling. Over the next half hour, they drank tea with some sort of brown liquid from a glass container added to it and shared more stories about small actions to make the town better for the ordinary citizens who lived in it.

Eventually, the clock chimed, and they all sighed regretfully in unison. A modest measure from the bottle was poured for each of them, and they raised their cups for a toast. The man said, "To the noble Order of the Silver Griffins, and to those of us who remember it in thoughts, words, or deeds." They clinked their glasses and drank together.

Rath grinned. At last, he had a name for the symbol he'd seen in the alleyway. He scampered up the stairs and out the window, then slid down the cable to return to his trusty steed.

"Home, Max. Nothing bad here. Only good. Very good."

## CHAPTER TWENTY-FIVE

The pieces had come together unexpectedly quickly. Sloan's report corresponded to a buzz among the street soldiers Kayleigh was tracking. She'd been following several, mapping their travel and checking out their phone contacts, when they suddenly vanished. Their cell signals were gone and the routes they normally took abandoned. The tech had cursed fluently and violently before she explained to her boss that the possibility of the disappearance being a random occurrence was zero. Every single one of them had gone radio-silent at the same time.

Diana knew from previous experience what such silences portended. A text summoning Sloan to action gave them the when—tonight, after midnight. They still didn't have the what, though. Diana and Kayleigh had spent the day in conference with ARES DC, and Bryant joined them from Hartford while he waited for a flight south. It was Tony who actually broke the case, so to speak. He devoted his afternoon to conferencing with the Pittsburgh Police, where he overheard a request for some officers to work overtime closing down highway accesses. His ears perked up when the man complained that the gig involved working with the feds.

He chatted to a few people and finally heard that a government transport—"some secret military thing"—was passing through town after midnight on the line to Chicago. He kicked that back to Diana, who put the ARES team on it. It took an hour to ferret out the details. A magic artifact had been discovered and identified by military mages as something of immense power. As usual, the army had chosen to keep it for its own. They had previously reconditioned the "white train" of the era of nuclear proliferation, turned it to a fortress on rails, and decided it would make a worthy carriage for the valuable find. Not only that, it would traverse Pittsburgh, home of the Remembrance who coveted magical artifacts, within thirty minutes of the time Sloan was to appear at the library for the heist.

Diana had put the call out to summon the whole team, and they arrived while she worked with Kayleigh to nail down the particulars of the scenario. ARES DC feared another coordinated attack and had put all their people on standby. A couple of hours before Sloan's deadline, there were credible rumors about attacks in both DC and Hartford, in addition to the one they knew about in Pittsburgh. The Cube shifted to high alert, and the FBI mobilized to assist in the surveillance and protection of government buildings in all the cities. She'd even paid a Willen to carry a message to Nylotte to request that she warn Lady Alayne, just in case.

The upshot was that handling the seemingly inevitable

attack had become the responsibility of Diana and her team. The Army's version of AET wasn't close enough to intervene and planned to intercept the train for escort in Cleveland. A call to suggest the transport be stopped received only derision. The army was convinced its protections would be more than adequate. Taggart made an impassioned argument against that position while Diana listened in, but he failed to convince the general on the other end. He ended the connection after the officer hung up and uttered a terse, "This one's on you, Sheen. Get it done."

She'd shared that word with her team, and they didn't flinch. The arming space felt a little tighter now with four agents, a troll, and a tech. Sloan was already on his way to the library heist. Kayleigh offered frequent updates on the police's actions, the progress of the train, and whatever else she could use to fill in the silences that might otherwise become nervous.

*She's way deeper and smarter than she lets people see. It's unfortunate. I wonder why she hides it.*

But the blonde would have to remain a mystery for another day. Tonight, there were criminals who needed their undivided attention.

"So, this promises to be an adventure, my friends. The army won't stop the train for us, because their orders are not to halt until Chicago, and by God, that's exactly what they'll do." Her imitation of the general's gruff voice brought laughs from her team. "Which, I guess, I can respect. They think they have it under control. If we're lucky, they do, and we're merely extra insurance."

Tony laughed. "When was the last time we were lucky, boss?"

Cara raised an eyebrow at him. "Maybe if you worked out more and shaved that caterpillar off your lip, your chances of getting lucky would improve."

He stared at the ceiling and sighed. "Abuse. All I get is abuse."

Diana gave him a shallow nod of appreciation for keeping the meeting light-hearted. "We'll go in by helicopter." Heads snapped around at that statement, and she nodded. "I told you all that taking this job would be an adventure. Well, tonight, if the Remembrance does what we think they will, you'll get to fly."

Rath clapped his hands. "Is good. I feel the need." Anik joined him unexpectedly to finish the quote. "The need for speed." The troll hopped on his bench so his three-foot form could reach the man for the usual fist bump. A pair of timers glowed in Diana's glasses and counted down. The smaller one measured the minutes to the helicopter pickup on the roof of the building. The second reflected when the train would be clear of the city so they could shadow it.

They'd discussed the options, and while the Remembrance could launch their attack sooner, it didn't make sense for them to do so. The run from Pittsburgh to Cleveland was through farmland, distant from major roads, and generally a suitable place to stage an action. In short, it was not a matter of if they would strike there but rather where and when along the stretch.

A text from Lisa scrolled into the right side of her glasses. A bunch of cartoon hearts melted into a picture of the three of them at the ballgame. She laughed and grabbed her phone, then sent back a kissing emoji before she stowed the device in the protected case on her belt.

Kayleigh moved from agent to agent and handed out the small boxes that Diana had requested. They were metal, about the size of a Zippo, and held four pills. Each stimulant was good for thirty minutes or so and impacted the system like caffeine but without the shakes. They weren't downside-free, though. The meds resulted in a brutal crash when they faded, but for late-night ops, they were handy to have on the off chance one started to feel a little woozy.

Based on the look of her team, however, they wouldn't need them. They were riding high on a crest of pent up expectation. Each wore basic ARES gear, although Tony had added a second pistol at his left hip in exchange for the pair of grenades that usually rode there. Kayleigh had promised to find a way to add them again at a later date and extra magazine loops had been fitted on his belt as a result, which caused the holders to look more crowded than Batman's utility belt. Diana had chosen a flash bang and a sonic for her left leg and a frag grenade at her belt.

Every agent, plus Rath, also wore a flight harness that looped over legs, waist, and shoulder and met at a large carabiner at their navels for the helicopter deployment. Heavy helmets would serve as protection while airborne. The troll's custom version had been 3D-printed for the occasion, thanks to Kayleigh's foresight. Each team member also carried a palm-sized square that contained a computer interface. If they found something to plug one of its four different connectors into, the tech would have an advantage in trying to break into an enemy system. They didn't know if they'd need it, but again, it was better to have it in case.

Diana wore her new, strangely heavy collar at the base of her neck. She'd asked about the danger of lightning, but naturally, the tech had already thought of that. A small cable connected it to the vest's absorption line. The others didn't have theirs yet, which Diana privately considered a good thing. It was better to test the gear in advance with only her as the guinea pig.

*It seems like I get to be everyone's experimental subject.*

Her leather bracelet with Nylotte's charms encircled her right wrist above the illusion detection one. She crossed the room to stand beside the core and faced away from the rest of her team. "Time to go to work, Friday."

The command activated the collar, and the AI's voice spoke through her earbuds. "Agent Friday reporting for duty." Diana groaned and hoped Kayleigh hadn't added in too many other surprises for her to find in interaction with the system. "Activate comms." A soft bell chimed to let her know the request had been received and executed successfully. "Comms check."

The other members of her team spoke one by one to confirm that their earphones and mics functioned properly. Diana toggled the switch to turn off her outgoing communication. "Show me the roof." Another chime sounded as a split window opened in her glasses to display the feed from the cameras mounted atop the building. There was nothing to see but darkness and the lights that marked the corners. The timer showed fifteen minutes until the helicopter would arrive, so that was to be expected. "Close it."

It would take some getting used to, but the new system had impressive promise. She turned to her team who were all ready to go. They carried equal amounts of hollow-point and anti-magic ammunition for their pistols and carbines since they didn't know what mix of enemies they'd have to face. She sat beside Rath as he strapped his vest on and secured the belt around his waist. "Are you up for this, champ?"

The troll grinned. "Never been on a train."

"Well, this isn't quite the way most people ride a train. They usually stay on the inside."

"More fun like this."

She laughed and drew him into a quick hug. "You keep being you, Rath, and there's no way we can lose."

He disengaged and did a backflip, landed in an exaggerated martial arts stance, and made a silly kung fu movie noise. Diana pointed at him as she stood. "You need to watch less television."

"Never. Max likes it."

"Uh-huh. Max. Sure."

He grinned and shifted into a new pose and she chuckled as she turned away to address the rest of the team.

"I don't have any fancy words for you. We have a job to do. Fortunately, it involves keeping scumbags from getting what they want, which has to be the best job ever. Grab your weapons and get to the roof. I'll be with you in a moment."

They nodded and departed, and she joined Kayleigh in the core. Three of the panels showed drone feeds, one of which flew above a locomotive. Diana gestured toward it. "Where's our target now?"

The other woman looked at another monitor, waved her hands, and a map appeared to reveal the train on the eastern side of the city. "It'll be in town in about ten minutes and out of town right on schedule. My best guess is that they'll attack about fifteen minutes after that to give them the most time from when it leaves a crowded place to when it returns to one, near Youngstown. They could also strike after that, of course, which would be a real pain in the ass. I hope the chopper has extra fuel."

Diana chuckled. "I'm sure they've handled those details. You don't have to worry about everything yourself."

The tech frowned at her. "Of course, I do. That's my job."

She touched her arm. "You're one in a billion. Stay with us."

"Ooh. Dirty play, boss. Going for the emotional hook. Not cool." They both laughed. "Talk to me after, assuming you manage not to crash the helicopter and the train and wind up in the hospital."

She smirked as she strode toward the elevator. "One of us, blondie."

Kayleigh's voice was clear in her earpieces as the lift door closed. "Worst. Fate. Ever."

Diana cracked her knuckles under her shock gloves.

*Let's teach some slimeballs about the dangers of causing trouble in our town.*

# CHAPTER TWENTY-SIX

The helicopter swooped in from the point where the rivers met and nosed up to hover above the rooftop. Two black ropes snaked out to puddle on the tarred surface and the team used the knots for a scrambled ascent into the aircraft. When they were aboard, Tony and Cara pressed the switches to retract the lines, and the chopper banked away. Scant moments later, they reached the tracks along the river and the aircraft aligned itself above the train's route. The interior of the cabin was crowded, although the benches on the front and back walls proved sufficient to seat all of them. Anik chose to stand and gripped the roof handles to maintain his balance.

"Friday, connect to the helicopter comms." After the soft bell, Diana said, "Status update?"

The pilot was a woman judging by the timbre of her voice. "Clean pickup. Good work. The target is ahead of us. We'll keep our distance at a mile and a half to the rear, as instructed."

"Excellent. Let me know if there's any change."

"Affirmative."

Diana silenced her feed momentarily using the glove stud. "Friday, listen-only on the helicopter." The soft bell chimed again, and she toggled her mic on. "Kayleigh, how are we doing?"

"There's no noise about the chopper on the normal channels. A couple of conspiracy theorists we're watching mentioned something on Twitter, but nothing big."

Tony's laugh intruded into the conversation. "Are you saying Twitter is inconsequential?"

Kayleigh's scorn was obvious. "Let's simply say that some of the people there don't exactly wisely choose who to listen to and leave it at that."

Cara added, "Instagram is where it's at. Have you seen Jason Momoa's feed?" She growled appreciatively.

Anik's calm tones carried an undertone of humor. "So, is this how y'all prep for missions? Social media discussions to make everyone angry enough to shoot?"

The investigator laughed again. "No, Cara merely has a thing for muscles."

Kayleigh purred. "Who doesn't?"

"Okay, people." Diana shook her head. "Time to put our game faces on." The banter subsided. "How's our timing?"

"On target, boss," the tech responded crisply. "Thirty seconds either way is the predicted boundary right now."

"Do you see any sign of them?"

Three windows opened in her visual field, each showing the feed from a drone. The other woman explained rapidly. "The left one is traveling about five minutes ahead of the engine. There's no activity there. The second is over the midpoint of the train. That's the highest, to avoid detection, and there's nothing to see there, either. The third is trailing behind you by a minute, so we'll have a warning if they come from that way. No action is evident so far." Each view remained in constant motion as the drones' cameras gimbaled three-sixty-degrees and tilted from horizontal to vertical and back. To look too long was nauseating, so Diana closed her eyes.

*For now, we have nothing to do but wait.*

After a couple of minutes, Cara broke the silence. "This is boring."

The team laughed and even Diana couldn't hold in a chuckle. "Right?"

Rath spoke unexpectedly. "Know anything about Silver Griffins?"

Before she could ask Friday to pull the information, Kayleigh responded. "I'm a huge fan of them, Rath. How did you hear of them?"

He sounded reluctant. "Someone mentioned them."

The tech must have picked up on his tone because she didn't pursue it. "Well, basically, before ARES, before the PDA, and before AET, they stood against bad magic on Earth. They ultimately disbanded and the members integrated into other government agencies."

Rath nodded and his helmet bobbed. "Good guys. Like us."

"You know it."

"Is excellent."

Diana wondered what had brought that on, but a set of three chimes from the AI distracted her. "Go, Friday."

The computerized woman's voice was soft but direct,

much like the on-screen version. "Notable activity on drone two."

"Show us." The window that displayed surveillance of their target expanded to fill her vision and presumably did the same on all the team's displays. Several military-style trucks had pulled beside the train on a long empty stretch. The timing was squarely within what they'd anticipated. "Can you get closer?"

"Stand by," Kayleigh said. The drone swooped lower, and the image came into better focus. Four canvas-topped vehicles bowled along the flat land on either side of the slight rise of the tracks. They loomed black against the darkness and traveled without headlights. According to the map the tech had added to Diana's display, a crossing a couple of miles ahead would force them to break off and reposition or risk collision with stopped traffic.

She straightened. "Okay, people. Here we go. Friday, include helicopter comms." She paused to allow the crew to join the feed, then continued. "They're making their move. It's time to make ours."

"Affirmative." The chopper's nose dipped slightly as the pilot accelerated sharply to close the gap. The plan was for the chopper to match the train's velocity and hold there as the BAM Agents descended using the ropes. Only a few of them, not including Diana, could have accomplished the touch-and-go deployment that would have been optimal.

*Well, it's almost touch and go, anyway. Landing on a train wouldn't be smart outside of an action film. I bet Rath would love it, though.*

She pointed decisively. "Anik, Cara, get ready to toss the lines." They unspooled the rope from its holder and looped it on the floor with one foot in the middle to keep it in place. That done, they attached heavy magnets to the bottom with a carabiner.

"Thirty seconds," the pilot reported. "The wind is good so this shouldn't be a problem." In the display, the canvas covers peeled off the frames to reveal a sizable number of humanoids, some definitely large enough to be Kilomea. Several vaulted onto the train, seemingly assisted by magic-users in the vehicles. They threw lines to the wizards, witches, and others who remained in the trucks and hauled them aboard.

The secure cars were identical heavily armored, windowless boxes. These had a door at each end and broad ones on the sides that were currently closed. Flatbeds broke the symmetry at intervals, carrying securely lashed crates in most cases. Rath had declared during the planning session that he wanted there to be a tank, but the closest thing the train offered was a Humvee with a machine gun on top.

The raiders had boarded the third car from the back. Flatbeds alternated with full cars toward the engine, and those behind were the standard heavy-duty safes on wheels. A bright flash stabbed through the darkness as a magic user cast a spell and the invaders disappeared into the hole that had been created in the roof of the train car.

The pilot jerked Diana's awareness back to the interior of the helicopter. "Stand by. Matching speed...now."

She breathed deeply. "Careful, people. Go." Cara and Anik flung the lines and shuttled down. When they reached the top of the train, they activated the magnets and the pilot spooled the lines back until they were mostly taut to provide stability for the others. Their descent went smoothly, and they took off their helmets and attached them to the lines, releasing the magnets so the chopper could retract the ropes and veer away. It would remain close, but the aviator couldn't do much for them at this point.

They'd landed on the tail car, as planned. "Kayleigh, do you have any insights for us?" Diana asked.

"None. There is thermal shielding on the cars and obviously no windows. I have nothing."

Diana shrugged. "Fast and hard, then, people. Rath, you're with me. We'll head to the one they broke into. The rest of you start at the back exactly as we planned to." They'd used an actual model train on the display table to determine the best tactics for the operation. The enemy's choice of boarding location had invalidated some of these, and the lack of intel had eliminated others. Unfortunately, that left them with only the most basic strategy—eliminating the marauders as they found them. The original tactic to start from the rear and sweep forward still applied, with the exception of two team members who would move forward to the section already boarded.

She triggered a private comms channel to Kayleigh as she made a running leap toward the car ahead and cleared the gap easily. "Have you had any luck getting the army to weigh in now that they've started the attack?"

"They welcome our assistance but lack the authority to tell us where anything on the train is. They've kicked it up the ladder."

"Once again, I am thankful we don't have such stupid bureaucracies in place. Keep me informed about anything I need to know out here in the real world." She launched onto the third car and stuck her head over the opening but yanked it back barely in time to avoid the gunfire from within.

Crouched low, she triggered the full communication channel again. "Rath, throw this in. Let's show them we're not playing around." He lobbed the fragmentation grenade she handed him into the hole, and she conjured a force shield over the opening. Loud clangs echoed as the grenade struck the barrier in the invaders' attempts to eject the explosive, rapidly followed by the inevitable conflagration and the shrapnel. She grinned as she lowered their defense and flipped inside, rolled as she hit, and raised her rifle.

Only a few enemies remained alive in the car. A wizard lay on the floor, his body shredded by shrapnel.

*I assume you were the one who threw it back at us. Stupid.*

A Kilomea lay crumpled in the corner, still alive but bleeding from a rash of wounds. Another wizard at the rear huddled behind a shield. Diana depressed the trigger on her weapon and delivered three anti-magic rounds into his chest. The man staggered against the wall of the car but didn't fall.

*Damn vests.*

He raised his wand and she yanked it from his hand with a telekinetic pull. He barely had time to register shock before Rath bounded in and performed a more literal assault when he jabbed the man hard in the thighs with his batons. The mage fell, and the troll zip-tied him.

Diana announced "Car three, clear. No obvious treasures. Moving forward."

---

Cara spoke softly into her mike from her place at the rear. "Ready to breach car one." Anik stood from where he'd knelt to attach a set of explosives on the latch side of the door. The low platform at the back was only large enough for the demolitions expert, so the others clung to the ladders on both sides and waited for him to provide entry.

He climbed away and nodded

"Blow it," Cara ordered,

The loud explosion as the charges detonated was muffled by their earpieces, and the door swung open. Cara was the first one in and sidestepped immediately to the left. Two stunned men in mismatched dark fatigues and body armor spun to face her and she studied them quickly. Their faces hosted sloppy beards and mustaches, their shirts were unbuttoned too low, and their boots were unaccountably dirty. Obviously, these were the targets. There was none of the efficient military look about them

There were too many innocents around and she went to standard protocol, firing a triple-tap of standard ammunition into each of their chests, knocking them back. She realized too late they were wearing vests.

Their rifles fired as they stumbled, and her vest caught a round as she lurched aside. Anik entered behind her and added more shots to each man in tightly grouped clusters that hurled them into the wall where they slumped awkwardly. Cara reached for the handle to open the exit, but her teammate put his hand on hers and shook his head.

He retrieved a device she hadn't seen before from a pouch on his thigh. Her look must have betrayed her thoughts because he spoke quietly as he set it against the door. “It’s a sniffer. If there are explosives on the other side, it’ll warn us. It doesn’t work on grenades, unfortunately. If it were me, I’d have put traps down.”

She nodded. “That makes sense.”

Anik pulled it back and frowned. “There’s nothing obvious.”

Cara pointed at a stack of heavy crates. “Rig a line. We can pull the door open from behind these.”

He stuck an adhesive hook on the floor and threaded a thin metal cable through it, attached the line to the door, and joined the others behind the barrier before he yanked sharply. The door opened and a grenade clattered, then detonated to ignite several boxes and canvas covers. Tony snatched a wall-mounted extinguisher as the other man jumped the gap to the small platform on the rear of the next car and repeated the process of demolishing the lock.

This time, the detonation wasn’t as much of a shock to those inside, and a hail of bullets greeted them as soon as it swung open. Cara and Tony retreated behind the metal walls of car one, and Anik lobbed a grenade into the other with a quiet, “Flash out.” It exploded and released light, sound, and concussion through the metal box. The gunfire neither slowed nor stopped.

*What the hell?* Cara realized that the only explanation involved some kind of magical protection, which made entry a real risk. She frowned, considered their options, and grinned. “Ready to breach car two. Here’s what we’ll do.”

# CHAPTER TWENTY-SEVEN

Diana had listened in when Cara and Anik rigged the line to exit the car and approved the plan. Her strategy had to be a little different, though. She and Rath ducked behind protective stacks of various supplies before she peered around and pulled down using her telekinesis. This time, the trap was a frag grenade that sprayed shrapnel toward them. The one piece that made it through the crates was slowed enough that it bounced off her vest with hardly a jolt.

She stared across the gap to the car on the other side. "It sure would be nice if we had an armed drone to demolish that door for me."

Kayleigh groaned. "Stop. Cara, say nothing." The ex-Marshall's chuckle was tease enough. "You're magical. Do magic."

Diana shrugged. *Good point.* Her lessons with Nylotte hadn't yet provided the key to drawing on her full power reserve, but she had learned to make the most of what she already had. She closed her eyes, focused, and willed all the force magic she had to coalesce in her right hand. Once she'd formed it into an orb the size of a softball, she gestured gently toward the car ahead. The ball hurtled forward with all the energy of her power and telekinesis behind it and punched through the handle, the lock above it, and part of the wall.

Rath clapped approvingly. "Nice shot."

She looked at her palm, a little surprised. "It was more powerful than I expected, but I suppose that's a good problem to have." She brushed her hands against one another. "Ready?" The troll nodded. "Okay, I'll yank it open and lead. Rifles first, magicals second, Kilomea third." He confirmed with another brusque nod. Diana yanked the door wide magically and raced toward the opening.

Automatic weapons' fire erupted through the entry. Her force shield protected her when it absorbed the impacts and bounced the bullets off to clatter on the metal floor. She hurdled the gap, slid into the fourth car, and thrust her magical barrier forward to batter the two gunmen who had opened fire. The energy wave propelled them into the unyielding wall at the far end, and bones crunched distinctively as they fell and their rifles clattered away.

Diana had a moment to enjoy it before new assaults struck her from behind.

The first was ice. She could tell by the haze that formed around her when the attack pounded home and was consumed by her anti-magic deflectors. Two of them blackened immediately. She realized that the second blow had landed as well when her third deflector shattered and the fourth darkened. She dove behind a nearby stack of uniformly stenciled military crates. Rath skidded into the car as she ducked securely behind cover. His feet thumped on the metal floor and he reached her in time for her to cast a shield to protect him from a repeat of the same bombardment. Ice and darkness flowed past the barrier she conjured.

*Shadow. Why does there always have to be so much shadow?* When a rare nightmare stole her sleep, it was invariably in the form of dark misty tentacles that pursued her, snatched at her, and squeezed the life from her. Her inner voice interjected with its usual snark, and she pictured herself standing with arms folded and a condescending look on her face.

*Perhaps a traumatic incident in your past? You know, therapy is good for that.*

*Shut up, you. I'm busy here. And you're apparently too stupid to recognize a rhetorical question.*

Mental Diana flipped her off and vanished.

The internal conversation banished any fear, and she glanced quickly at Rath. She held an open palm up and counted down from five. When she closed her fist, they moved. The enemy saw her first when she stepped into the aisle created by the storage boxes while the troll still clambered up and over the obstruction he'd taken cover behind. She thrust a hand at a witch on the left and a wizard on the right. Her telekinesis failed to steal the wand from her first opponent, but it did delay the woman's attacks. Diana's force bolt met the ice blast in midair and spun shards like shrapnel in an expanding circle. She flinched when one sliced into her right cheek immediately below her eye. The wizard absorbed some of the blowback as well, and Rath made small yelp of excitement as he barreled toward the witch.

The distraction proved useful against the woman. Her effort to bring her wand to bear on the troll might have been in time but for the icy needles that struck her in the leg, torso, and ear and broke her concentration. Rath's two-footed kick connected with her face as she ducked to avoid the missiles and her skull connected with the metal behind her. Her eyes rolled back in her head as she sagged to leave a bloody smear on the wall. He landed cleanly, but shards of ice under his feet stole his balance and he flailed momentarily before he fell.

The wizard waved his wand in an arc to create a frozen barrier around him. Diana sensed the continuing magic as he reinforced it.

*Damn it. They're playing the delaying game again. I hate these people.*

She focused on raising the largest force blast she could and hurled it into the protective shield, but it failed to penetrate and the divot it made was quickly filled. Instinct made her reach within for fire, but as it always did in her exercises, the element still escaped her. She growled in frustration.

Rath clapped once and she turned in surprise. He pantomimed an arc in the air, and she glanced up with a smile. She nodded and cupped her hands as he flicked his batons out. He took three running steps in her direction and hopped onto her palms. She flung him to the apex of the barrier. The way he disappeared from view confirmed that the enemy had only thought in two dimensions and had left the top unguarded. Shouts of pain and the sharp cracks of the stun batons signaled the troll's success. A triumphant warrior soon climbed out of the makeshift shelter at a higher height and shrank back to his smaller size. "Great idea, buddy. Did you get their wands?"

"Yes." He produced them and passed them to her.

"Excellent."

She found cover and waited until he was protected as well before she used her magic to manipulate the handle of the exit door. There was no reaction, and she peered carefully around the corner. The next car was a flatbed filled with enemies of every sort—Kilomea, wizard, witch, and mundane weapon-wielders. One of them stood at the center and pointed his wand down at the tracks.

*Bloody hell.*

---

Cara assumed that wizards supported the riflemen in car two, based on the way the flashbang had failed to stop the incoming barrage. Now, each agent held a grenade. Tony had a sonic, which might drive its attack unhindered through a physical shield. Cara had chosen pepper, which could potentially curl through the cracks in any defense. Anik gripped a frag grenade, which he would pitch in first. He had complained that he wouldn't hit anyone if the defenses were up, but that was the point. She wanted the mages to focus on defending against the first grenade in the hope that the distraction would leave crevices in their protection against the others. It was divergent thinking, to say the least.

She took a centering breath. "Go, Anik."

The man threw his grenade and ducked behind the cover of car two's metal wall, his feet sure and balanced on the small platform. She waited for the space of two heartbeats and gave her next signal. "Go, Tony," she ordered and flung hers at the same time. Their grenades were still in flight when the first detonated. As the second wave erupted, the fusillade from men, Kilomea, and magicals faltered, and she barreled ahead with Tony a couple of steps behind her as she cleared the gap between the cars.

She'd been wrong about her assumption about the wizards. They were actually witches if one were to demand specifics in the heat of battle. The enemies were arranged with the magicals on the outside and the gunmen on the inside a step back. All four women coughed, sputtered, or moaned from the effects of the grenades. It was quick work to disable the enemy after that. Soon, they were lined up and bound with zip-ties. Anik looked up from where he worked to secure the final prisoner and grinned. "That was too easy. Good plan."

Diana's voice startled them all. "Get to the roof, fast. Kayleigh, get the chopper in here. They intend to separate the cars."

The tech's voice replied a moment later. "Thirty seconds out."

It took a moment for the gravity of that report to sink in before the three agents responded to their boss' warning and exploded into action. Cara was first out the door and clutched the rungs on the right ladder to climb to the roof. Anik took the left. Vibrations from below told her the detective was close on her heels. In other circumstances, she would have voiced a taunt, but this wasn't the time. She made it to the top, raised her rifle, and aimed ahead but found no targets as she walked steadily toward the center.

The others soon clambered up behind her. Tony saw the chopper first. "There it is," he said. The black aircraft was only visible in the darkness by the blinking lights that were doubtless for their benefit. The sound of the rotors rolled over her ears moments after, and despite her lack of knowledge of helicopters, it definitely seemed to be in a hurry. With a distinctive crackle, the pilot's voice joined the comms channel.

"It looks like we need to do this fast. I have two lines out. Someone will have to climb up first."

"There's no time to waste," Kayleigh added briskly. "Diana is blocking them, but it'll only work for a few seconds more before they find an angle to hit her."

Anik tapped Cara on the shoulder. "You probably want to do the hero thing and go last, but you have the best skill to jump and scramble up. Fortunately, I'm a big enough person to admit this. I'll keep an eye on the front and jump on after you."

She frowned but pushed down her automatic dismissal of the idea.

*Damn it, he's right.*

With a curt nod, she moved into position across from Tony, who faced the back of the train on the left. The detective looked nervous and she flashed her teeth in a reassuring grin. "Easy peasy, fellas. Grab the rope and don't let go. There's no need to climb too high since we'll be off again shortly."

Tony's face was locked somewhere between panic and exhilaration, which seemed like an entirely reasonable response given the circumstances. The wind picked up as the helicopter dipped and pulled its nose up to swing the ropes toward them. The heavy-duty carabiners glinted in the moonlight. Cara crouched and vaulted upward to seize her line several feet up and focused on nothing more than getting higher. The cable jerked when Anik caught it a moment later, and she looked down to where he held on with both hands. His boots dangled awkwardly.

He saw her expression and gave a small laugh. "I'm good. For a while, at least. It's not your fault. The rope jerked right before I caught it."

As she spun on the line, she peered into the darkness around them and said a quiet prayer to the universe that they'd make it in time to help Diana and Rath.

# CHAPTER TWENTY-EIGHT

Diana held the barrier for as long as she could, but keeping it directional to protect the connection between the cars left her open to attack. She deflected a rifle with her telekinesis to force the shots to fire wide, then jerked a wand out of the line, but her efforts would ultimately prove futile. The rapid thump-thump of the chopper assured her that her teammates had secured their ride, but she was once again forced to duck behind the door. A giant fireball washed into the car, which lurched as the steady pull from the front vanished.

She screamed, "Rath, go!" and followed him onto the small platform at a sprint. The gap between the cars widened with every precious second, and the enemies on the flatbed were incredibly pleased by their success, judging by the looks on their faces. The troll jumped at an angle to the right, and his acrobatic talent was such that he would make it even though his trajectory wasn't direct.

Her own skills were less adequate, so her only option was through. She launched herself across the space and folded her body into a shield of force. Her path rocketed her directly at the mage who had thrown the fireball as his wand came forward to cast again. The vicious flames wound around her, and the increased temperature made her vision swim. Thankfully, her defense held.

The rumble of the helicopter became a distant sound as she careened into the wizard and thrust him off his feet. Her head struck his unintentionally, which left her a little dazed, but she had enough presence of mind to scramble away and regain her footing. She raced for the only cover she could find—the Humvee strapped down across the train car. Bullets pounded into the metal as she skidded around it for cover. Several of the projectiles found the back of her body armor and pitched her forward onto her face. Survival instinct kicked in and she floundered toward the tire without conscious thought. She sat with her spine against the vehicle and used the wheel for cover and used the brief respite as she tried to gather her wits.

Yells and more weapons' fire preceded another telltale whoosh of flame. Rath appeared around the rear corner of the car at a run. "Too many," he panted. "Get up." He yanked both grenades from his bandolier and threw them one after the other over the top of the vehicle. Frantic shouts were cut off when the canisters detonated, causing a lull in the relentless fusillade.

The troll scampered over and studied her face with concern. "Diana. Healing potion?" His anxious expression penetrated where the rest of the surrounding action had not, and she shook her head. "I'm good, Rath. I only need a minute."

His expression was grim. "No time. Flanking."

She nodded and lurched to her feet with a groan. "I'd say we should make a break for it since these assholes are trying to slow us down, but leaving them at our backs would be a bad idea."

The troll grinned. "Have plan. Keep them busy."

Diana shrugged. *It's not like I have any better ideas at the moment.* She clambered onto the hood of the Humvee to give the enemy a clear target and summoned a force shield that extended in a curve to both sides. It stretched from the body of the vehicle to just over the top of her hair. Magic battered it instantly but the flame was unable to penetrate, and for once, no shadow tentacles appeared to torment her. Another witch thrust a blast of force out, but it failed to pierce her defenses. Bullets peppered the barrier in a steady beat and each added to the throbbing in her head, but she gritted her teeth and fed more power to the shield.

*Come on, Rath. Whatever you have planned, do it.* She gestured, and the clasp on one of the straps securing the goods to the flatbed flicked open. The crates it had restrained slid across the surface, inward and back, and her enemies paused their attacks in order to protect themselves.

She redirected a crate's momentum enough to sweep it into a witch on the far side and jolt her off the edge of the train. Her mouth froze in a horrified scream that was drowned out by the noise of the wind and the tracks.

Diana targeted a rifleman on the other side and flicked at his knee to make it buckle, then pushed him outward as well. He fell frantically to his stomach to avoid tumbling off.

*All right, now we're getting somewhere.*

Suddenly, the world decelerated, and her vision expanded to the now familiar panorama. A new enemy emerged beyond the outline of the Humvee and she noted his peculiar behavior absently. The man was a wizard she hadn't seen before. He crouched low to the ground and had apparently crawled under the vehicle while she was occupied with the others. His wand was pointed at her, and his lips moved. She did the only thing she could think to do and backflipped off the hood.

A burst of light energy streaked through the place where she had stood. The slow motion threw off her sense of balance given the fast motion of the train, though, and she stumbled when she landed and fell hard enough for it to hurt. She only realized her real danger when her head failed to connect with the flatbed and the wind surged into one of her eardrums. Panicked, she flailed her right hand in search of anything at all to take hold of, and her magic saved her again. A thin line of force emerged and whipped out to wind around the enemy's legs. She yanked forcefully, and the effort simultaneously pulled herself onto the platform and flung him onto his back. His wand spun free when she flicked her left fingers and time snapped into its normal speed.

Diana drew her pistol and fired three shots at his chest. All of them missed and he scrambled to his feet. She sighted carefully, fired again. and continued to pull the trigger until the gun locked open, but with no success. The bullets struck the vehicle beside him instead. She holstered her weapon as she bolted toward him, clutched his shirt, and drove a fist into his face. The blow would have been adequate on its own, but the sparking shock that accompanied it put him down like his bones had evaporated.

Diana stumbled to one knee and looked around. *Where the hell is Rath?*

---

It had taken the troll what felt like an eternity to open the door of the Humvee. He'd had to grow halfway between his medium and large sizes to do it and had lost all his gear in the process. Once that was accomplished, he'd had to identify how to start it, which turned out to be a lever on the left, not the expected key. The inside was dark since blast shields were down over each of the windows, and it took him even longer to locate the release for the sunroof.

But find it he did, and he flipped the cover open quietly while he kept his head down. No gunfire ensued, so he assumed the action remained a secret. He found the safety for the machine gun mounted on the top and released it. A deep breath steadied him before he stood, seized the handles of the heavy machine gun, and swung it sideways toward the enemy. Both thumbs pressed the trigger, and his arms shook as the ammunition belt fed from the box on the left of the weapon and spent shells left the barrel. He fired in short bursts, but the unfamiliarity of the weapon made him miss most of his intended targets.

Part one of his goal was accomplished, however, since the surprise attack drove the enemy into cover. As he learned better control of the machine gun, Rath chewed away at their protection. He swept the bullets to the right, which forced one foe to choose between being shot and leaping off the train, which he did with a scream and flailing arms that the troll found amusing.

Counterfire ricocheted off the shield on either side of the thin slit he aimed through, and he searched for the shooter. The wash of flame that followed drove him into the vehicle, and he paused for a moment in fear of an explosion. When moments passed without further danger, he darted up and pressed the trigger down to hose the platform indiscriminately until the ammunition feed ran dry. He abandoned the vehicle in a forward leap and changed to full size as he landed.

The shell-shocked enemy had yet to come to terms with having been fired at by a troll with a machine gun, and he used their distraction to his advantage. His first target was the fire mage, and he threw her bodily from the train. The attack she'd launched burned the skin on his left arm and leg, but he growled through the pain and pushed on. A man to his right raised a rifle, and Rath delivered a rapid sidekick that hurtled him off the car to the opposite side. The troll laughed and shouted, "Rath smash!" before a force bolt caught the back of his shoulder.

He spun, crouched, and launched himself at the wizard who was only a short distance away. His adversary fell with the violent tackle and Rath rolled to get his feet under the man's body and heaved him into a flip. The hapless man struck a passing tree, and his assailant winced.

*Ouch. Had to hurt.*

He rose and peered around suspiciously, but their adversaries were gone—either defeated, fled, or vanished. Still alert and watchful, he circled the Humvee toward where he'd last seen Diana and found her slumped against the vehicle. He rushed to her side, snatched the healing potion from her waist, and shoved it into her hand.

She shook her head and mumbled, "I don't need this." Rath simply pushed the hand closer to her mouth. She apparently realized that arguing with an almost eight-foot troll wasn't a great idea because she drank without protest. The results were immediate, and she blew out a heavy breath.

"Thanks. I needed that."

He nodded and tapped his head. "You got scrambled."

She laughed. "Yes. Yes, I did. But I'm better now. Are you okay?"

He showed her his arm, which was only lightly injured. "Little burn. No biggie." He offered her the other one, and she used it to climb slowly to her feet before she latched the empty potion vial onto her belt.

Diana paused and gazed in all directions to get her bearings. "Kayleigh, status on the chopper?"

The tech exhaled an explosive sigh of relief. "Forty seconds out. They had to pull back when the train passed through a short tunnel. So did the drone. We don't have eyes on you at the moment."

She laughed. "That's okay. I'm not much to look at right now."

"The army finally got back to us. There's an artifact several cars ahead. If you're where I think you are, there should be a storage car and a flatbed between you and it."

"Got it."

"They're putting together an assault team to board the train after it gets through the next town, so you'll have a little help."

"Yeah, I imagine that'll be too late." She sighed. "It's probably already too late. These bastards have tried to slow us down again like they always do."

Cara shouted over the wind that filled the channel when she activated her mic. "You'd think we'd have learned by now. Someone should talk to the person in charge."

The insult made her smile, then laugh. "Bite me, Cara. Maybe once you're done with your little vacation, you could get back in the game?"

"Only if you promise to leave some for me."

"Done."

She stood and studied the car ahead. "There's no time like the present, Rath."

"The game is afoot." She stared at him, and he shrugged. "Get a move on, Watson." She shook her head, laughed at him, and threw a blast of force at the locked door ahead.

## CHAPTER TWENTY-NINE

There was no incoming fire from the next car, so Diana summoned a force shield and thrust forward to land inside. The feeling of tiredness she'd often experience near the end of a training session with Nylotte crept up from within. She had been drained by the combination of the healing potion's pull on her systems and the enormous use of power thus far.

*There's no time to worry about that now.*

Her danger sense activated again and warned her of nearby magic, but she saw nothing at all. She held a hand out to stop Rath as she peered around, unable to identify the source even after several moments of intense focus. She pushed her will toward the bracelet Nylotte had given her and whispered, "Fortus sensus."

The charm came to life, and warmth rushed up her arm from her wrist. As it reached her ear, the sounds that had merged together suddenly separated into identifiable components—the *tick-tock* of the wheels on the rails and the *whop-whop* of the approaching helicopter. Beneath it all, her heartbeat kept time, and Rath's faster one provided a counter rhythm.

*This would be amazing at a concert.*

The awareness extended to her tongue and nose, neither of which were pleased with the increase in sensitivity. The skin on her face registered a trickle of air that hadn't been there before—perhaps from a break in the metal walls. When the warmth reached her eyes, Diana gasped. The smallest details were visible to her in a way that, if viewed as a whole, would have been a mishmash of color, texture, and motion. Each object she focused on came into perfect clarity and separated from the visual noise she'd never noticed before.

She scrutinized the car again and identified a shimmering wave in the middle of the space that radiated out along the floor from either side. It didn't look like any tripwire she'd ever seen, and then she realized that it pulsed in rhythm with a small hum at the edge of her hearing.

*Holy hell. I'm seeing sound.*

Time resumed its natural flow, which made the images harder to take in. She whispered, "Apstergo sensus," and her vision returned to normal, as did her other senses.

*Mental note: bring mints from now on.*

She shook her head, pictured a force shield, and built it in her mind before she stretched her hand out to call it into being. It raised into a high rectangle over the zones where she'd noted the patches and enclosed them and half the wall above them, then extended a couple of feet deeper into the car. She held the magic while she and her partner climbed over. They inched into the corner nearest the exit since they lacked cover to protect them if opening the door activated another trap. She was unwilling to release the barrier over what she suspected was a sonic tripwire of some sort.

Diana wrenched the exit open with her telekinesis, and it swung into the room. She peeked cautiously into the space beyond and saw only an empty flatbed ahead with a closed car directly ahead of it. *That's the one with the artifact, so that's where they'll be.*

She and Rath cleared the gap onto the bare platform, and she released her magic mid-flight. The air flooded through the open door and triggered the trap, and the metal box split in half as an explosion of magical energy surged through it. The flatbed rocked as the car behind it left the track, and Diana fired a force bolt at the connection as she landed to release the derailed portion to tumble off to the side. She exhaled slowly, then summoned the strength to advance, meet the enemy, and end the battle.

---

Cara looked at Anik, who maintained his grip gamely at the end of the cable but gritted his teeth as they flew ahead. The explosion of several train cars had left the pilot with little choice but to swerve, which set her passengers into an uncomfortable series of lurches and sways that made holding on more difficult. Tony gripped his rope tightly and closed his eyes as it swung alarmingly. Her stomach lurched, as much from watching his acrobatics as from her own, and she forced the nausea down. *Jump school is one thing. This is insanity.* She pressed the stud to activate her mic. "Flatbed ahead. Get us there. Now."

"On it," the pilot replied crisply. The helicopter's nose dipped as she accelerated. The lines leaned toward the rear of the aircraft with the wind resistance. Cara expected the woman to pull up quickly and swing them forward, then hover and allow things to settle before she lowered them farther. Unfortunately, that was not to be.

Below, Diana had released the enclosed car to tumble away, and Cara caught a flicker of something that didn't look quite right two-thirds of the way back on the flatbed. Her eyes widened when she realized what it had to be.

"Illusion," she shouted in the same moment that the concealment dropped to reveal several enemies ahead. While she recognized some from their fight at the Cube, others were new. All carried wands and pointed them directly at her boss.

"Get us down there right now, whatever you have to do." The ex-Marshall grasped the rope tighter and hoped that their teammates on the ground could keep the enemy at bay long enough for them to arrive.

---

Diana was stunned as the illusion vanished to reveal enemies ranged against her at the far end of the car and cursed her stupidity. It was something she should have considered, at least. She recognized the two dressed entirely in black immediately. The figure on the far left was the witch she'd last seen tumbling into the portal conjured by her fellow wizard. That man stood beside her and closest to the center. An arrogant smirk conveyed his satisfaction at having surprised her. Beside them stood three more wizards, all in various colored outfits. They brandished their wands threateningly.

"Rath, do you want another shot at the witch?"

He growled, which she took as an affirmative.

She shouted over the noise of the wind and tracks, "Can we talk about this?"

The enemy leader laughed and assumed a gloating expression that she much preferred not to stand and stare at. Instead, she charged the wizard farthest to her right. She summoned a ball of force and flung it at him sidearm, and the practice she'd had at the batting cages with Rath proved its value. The mage conjured his own force wave to deflect it, but she had managed to throw him slightly off balance. He crumpled as the telekinetic punch to the knee that followed flipped him over the edge.

Shouts of rage mingled with cries of loss as the temporary ceasefire turned into an all-out brawl. Attack spells rocketed at her from all angles. She dodged the shadow orbs with a diving tumble and rolled to her feet in time to meet a blast of lightning from the wizard on the end. This version was different than the kind she'd faced before. A confined cone of the magic had somehow connected to her. The spell channeled, rather than being consumed in a single strike. Her vest sparked, and the resistors popped in sequence as her muscles locked. She screamed and fell when her muscles spasmed.

Rath's assault led him directly to the enemy witch. One of the other wizards cast ice at his feet, but he'd had enough experience with that trick to avoid it easily. As he'd expected, the patch extended down the bed, so if he had continued straight, he would have slid off the train. He landed securely and his long legs ate up the distance as he lowered his body in readiness to pounce on his target.

Her face contorted in anger and disgust. Ice erupted from her wand and he ducked his head instinctively but the follow-up attack hammered into his shoulder. He whirled to continue his forward momentum and had to dodge once again as the wizard cast at him a third time. The troll surged ahead with the intention to pitch the smug woman off the platform like he'd sent her into the portal. Instead of the horror he'd expected, the woman looked at him with a chilling smile.

She extended her black-sleeved arms and his eyes locked on her wicked black nails as shadowy tentacles emerged from each of them. There was nothing he could do to defend himself in the split second before they encircled him. She yanked her arms down, and the appendages slapped him onto the platform with the speed of a whip. Their crushing force was brutal on the troll's body, and his struggles had no effect.

He wracked his brain for a way to escape, but his vision began to sparkle from a lack of breath. Dimly, he realized that he had nothing...no plan and no means of escape. He looked at Diana where she writhed on the ground and struggled to regain control of her body, and he yearned for her as the world began to swim. If this was the end, he wanted to be close to the woman he had come to see as family.

---

Diana had plunged deep inside herself as the lightning ravaged her. She did her best to ignore the burns that seared into her flesh and the havoc it wreaked on her muscles. Nylotte's voice echoed in her ears. "Reality exists only in the mind."

She took a deep breath and shut away the things she didn't want to think about—the pain, the frustration, worry for Rath...all of it. As she spiraled down, she pictured a lake of lava. The pool appeared and filled her with hope, and she thrust through it unexpectedly to discover a world beneath filled with storms, rain, thunder, and lightning.

It felt like she was underground, but she couldn't imagine a cavern large enough to contain the violent weather. She stretched her hands instinctively and drew the primal forces contained in the space into her, and the descent stopped, then reversed. Her pained retreat transformed into an energized purpose as she careened out of the mental cavern and prepared for battle.

*Round two, punks.*

Like a woman possessed, she launched to her feet and screamed. The lighting that wreathed her body now fueled her magic. Her arms swung wide to sweep it in a wave at her enemies, who could not react before they were struck and fell to thrash and flail in its deadly embrace. Rath stumbled upright and stood shakily beside her, and she extended the healing potion she carried for him. He drank quickly and rallied. The enemy moved slowly and fixed her with wary gazes as they, too, struggled back to their feet.

Diana shouted to be heard over the din. "You're under arrest. Come quietly or face the consequences of your decisions."

The witch cackled, and the enemy leader shook his head and yelled a defiant response. "You are not as powerful as you pretend to be. You can't defeat us all."

Three things happened in quick succession. First, the two enemies on the inside stepped away from the door to the train carriage behind them. Second, a pair of Kilomea followed by several normal-sized beings barreled out of the car.

*Damn it. I should have blasted them and been done with it, rather than giving them a choice.*

Third—and much better, from her point of view—the helicopter flew over and Cara, Tony, and Anik dropped and rolled into the empty space between the forces. Diana grinned at the sight of her team alive and presumably well.

*Now it's a party. Let's do this.*

"You three handle the trash. When you're done, give Rath a hand. I'm on the leader."

The troll yelled, "Luke, trust your instincts," as he dashed at the witch, and Diana's sprint at her own enemy was accompanied by laughter at his unbreakable spirit. She tried to steal the witch's wand as a way to distract her, but the woman turned it into an attack by using redirection to fire a bolt of ice at Diana's head. The agent slid on the metal, bent back to get under it, and straightened immediately when the danger passed. From the corner of her eye, she caught a brief glimpse of a satisfying sight when the troll plowed into his adversary and upended her perilously close to the edge of the platform.

Satisfied, she returned her focus to the battle and dodged more shadow orbs from the wizard ahead of her. "I think I've seen you somewhere before. Oh, yeah, that's right, you were running away like a coward."

He laughed. "And you were trapped in an exploding building. And yet, here we both are."

Her retort was forestalled by barbed tentacles that erupted from his torso like extra arms. The creepy appendages snatched hungrily at her. Not to be outdone, the witch sent her own grasping limbs at Rath, who dodged and wove among them with ease as he shrank down to his three-foot form. Diana conjured the force lariat she'd summoned the last time the wizard had tried that trick, and he repeated his defense when he banished the tangled limbs and called them back into being. She used the moment between to draw her Glock and squeezed the trigger as fast as she could. The anti-magic bullets pierced the tentacles he interposed as a shield without slowing, and he fell when they struck home in his chest and one arm.

Diana lurched forward to finish him but was distracted by a yelp from the right as Anik catapulted toward the back of the platform from a blow by another wizard. She used her telekinesis to slow him and created a sloped force barrier that drained the rest of his momentum as he slid up it. He dropped painfully to the surface, her control imperfect, but at least he hadn't fallen off. She turned to deal with his attacker in time to see Tony and Cara both fire at center mass. The caster stumbled over the edge and the speed of the train sucked him under the wheels. She winced at the thought of what would inevitably happen to that particular body.

Incoming tentacles appeared in her peripheral vision and she spun to roll out of the way. The witch used the opportunity to scamper into the doorway of the car ahead. Her writhing appendages scooped her leader up and pulled him in after her. The remaining Kilomea thrust into Diana's path as she moved to pursue. She pounded him with a force punch that knocked him aside, but he'd achieved his purpose.

Even as she raced forward to catch the woman, she saw the triumphant smile on her face as an ornate crate floated into a portal behind her. Diana yelled as she hurled a ball of force at the witch's head, and her adversary half-turned and frowned. Her shadow appendages twitched as she used the leader as a shield to intercept the orb. The missile struck his torso with a loud crack and dragged a gasping scream from him.

"Get us out of here!" he shouted,

Rath whipped past her and latched onto the man's foot. He swelled to full size and hauled with all his strength to prevent their enemies from escaping. For a moment, the witch seemed undecided, then she gave Diana a brilliant smile and ripped the wizard from Rath's powerful grasp. She hurled the man outward before she entered fully into the rift. The portal collapsed as Diana dodged the human missile, and she spun in readiness. He had landed on the platform and her teammates had already moved to secure him. She twisted back to stare at where her enemy had been and growled in frustration.

*That's twice you people have gotten away. There won't be a third time.*

# CHAPTER THIRTY

Kayleigh flicked a switch and a suit of armor appeared above the display table and rotated slowly in their AR glasses. The tech had been busy in the days following the incident on the train. And, judging by the constant flow of messages she'd sent Diana about the inadequacies of virtually every branch of government and the military, the woman was livid.

"After the army finally admitted what was taken—which required so many phone calls that I'm absolutely certain I set a new freaking world record—I approached the Oriceran Consulate for information. They weren't all that forthcoming, but Bryant was able to intervene, thanks to his daring rescue of the ambassador."

Diana's voice was incredulous. "His rescue? Rath and I almost died, and he says it was…" She trailed off as she noticed the vicious grin on her friend's face and snorted. "Oh, good one. I'll get you back for that." The others laughed, even those who only knew Bryant by reputation.

"Anyway, this gear is called Rhazdon's Defense. It

wasn't used by the leader but rather created from several artifacts by a number of mages with more skills than wisdom."

"Wait," Cara interjected. "Are you telling me this is one giant artifact?"

Kayleigh shook her head. "It's a collection of separate artifacts, as I understand it, that they've managed to convince to work together. While it's always been something of a fundamental truth that artifacts aren't willing to share a host, this is somehow different. Maybe because it's worn rather than embedded or whatever."

Diana groaned. "This stuff keeps getting worse. Do we know its powers?"

The tech shrugged. "Until now, it's essentially been treated as a myth. The army didn't know what they had, and it took the consulate a while to identify it too. They probably had to phone home for a historian or something."

Tony frowned. "They can call the other world on a phone?"

Cara turned to him and shook her head in disappointment. "Honestly, Tony, have you seen any movies at all? Ever?

He grinned. "*Tomb Raider*. I'm a fan of Angelina Jolie."

"Well, can't fault you there, but *Wanted* is more my speed."

He snapped his fingers. "That's it! Your callsign is Croft."

She rolled her eyes, but Anik nodded. "Yes, that fits. Definitely Croft."

Tony turned to him. "You're Khan, for sure."

"Hyper-intelligent perfect man? Of course."

The detective looked at Kayleigh thoughtfully. "You have like five times the fashion sense of Cara or Diana, and you have those awesome boots, so… Glitz? It's techie."

She scowled and Diana rescued him. "Glam. Much more Kayleigh's style." The tech thought about it for a second, then nodded.

Tony continued, obviously on a roll. "You'll be Boss, naturally, boss."

"That works. And I dub thee Stark for that ridiculous mustache and your general troublemaking attitude."

The detective laughed and nodded. "Fair enough." Finally, he turned to Sloan. "You're Face, of course."

Sloan nodded. He had been uncharacteristically subdued since he'd missed the attack on the train. Diana had chatted to him about it to be sure that he knew no one bore a grudge. Nonetheless, it still clearly bothered him to have been absent when the team could have used his skills, despite the fact that he'd used them for the team's benefit at the time.

*Emotions and logic rarely travel together.*

"How about Bryant?"

Diana waved her hand dismissively. "BC."

"Chucklehead," Cara countered.

"Doubleboss," Tony suggested.

Diana glared at him, and he shrugged helplessly. "What? You have to admit it fits."

Anik and Sloan were silent. Finally, a smile dawned on the tech's face. "Well, we have a Face. So, how about Hannibal?"

The whole team laughed.

"Howling Mad Murdock might be more appropriate," Diana said once they had settled.

The investigator shook his head. "One word only."

"Fine. Be that way. Hannibal it is."

Kayleigh grinned. "I love it when a plan comes together."

Diana clapped her hands. "Okay, we've been beaten twice by these assholes. Sure, they didn't get everything they wanted and we captured their leader, which are at least semi-wins. But they feel like losses." The others nodded their agreement. "It's time to find a way to eliminate them once and for all. Let's get to it."

## CHAPTER THIRTY-ONE

The day devoted to intense planning and strategic analysis had mentally drained everyone involved. Tony and Cara agreed that light competition at the shooting range would be exactly the thing to wake them up before dinner. She'd driven them there in one of the ARES SUVs, and they spent an hour practicing with revolvers, pistols, and carbines. He was still more proficient with the smaller weapons, but he had a long way to go before he could challenge her with a rifle.

They both felt considerably better about life as they strolled to the parking lot afterward. The sun was setting, and the dim illumination of the streetlights high above slowly began to kick in. The weather was perfect for the light-black denim coat she wore, one of her favorites that also hid her shoulder holster effectively. "You're really good with small weapons. I wonder why that is," she teased.

Tony laughed and smoothed his mustache. "Finesse.

Precision. You know, things you wouldn't understand. But it's okay. You can learn."

She shook her head with a smile. "You keep telling yourself that. A man who walks around in an untucked dress shirt has no right to claim finesse and is leagues away from style."

He shot her an offended glare and looked at his outfit. "There's no need to insult the clothes. That's past the line." He demonstrated the line and her going past it with a small set of gestures.

Cara barked a laugh. "Okay, where do you want to go to dinner?"

A fireball preempted his answer. She had briefly seen a reflection of the nondescript van that glided to a halt, which had been a subtle warning. The rasp as the door slid open had focused her attention, and the image of the trio of mages that scrambled out and raised their wands had precipitated a hasty dive to the side as she yelled, "Cover!"

Triple blasts of fire struck the SUV and hurtled it up and away. The vehicle tumbled in ungainly free-flight into a car farther down in the parking lot. It settled and the flames immediately spread.

She picked herself up and drew her Ruger but was forced to dodge a cone of flame. The mage shifted his aim and forced her to run to evade the continuous attack. She took a wild shot that accomplished nothing and angled her path in an attempt to move closer to them. A second cone appeared ahead of her, and the two swung toward her from opposite sides. She looked for a way out but found none in either direction as the missiles converged, so simply did what soldiers did best. She focused on the objective and turned toward the van to make her final shots count.

Tony ran forward with a noticeable limp and a pistol in each hand. He alternated shots, which forced the mages to abandon their attacks and summon shields, and the cones immediately faded with no power to sustain them. Their adversaries blocked the normal bullets from his automatic but failed against the anti-magic rounds in his second pistol. When his first round didn't drop the mage he'd targeted, the detective shifted his aim to kill him with a single headshot, then dispatched the second in the same way. The last man flung himself into the van and slammed the door behind him. The tires screeched as the vehicle fled. Unfortunately, Tony failed to hit the tires before it accelerated out of range.

Cara holstered her weapon and thrust out both hands with her fingers spread and palms down. Flaming darts erupted and rocketed at an angle toward the base of the vehicle. She managed definite strikes to the front and rear tires on the passenger side, and the van slewed wildly before it flipped and rolled. When it finally settled, they sprinted to the driver's seat. The man behind the wheel was unconscious, saved by his seatbelt. The mage hadn't been so lucky. His broken body lay in a crumpled heap on the van's ceiling.

She raised her watch and held her fingerprint against it for five seconds. The emergency function activated, and she said "Phalanx." Had she not spoken, every member of the team would have stopped what they were doing and rolled to her location except for Kayleigh, who would have coordinated with local authorities to do the same. The command instead warned everyone that they needed to hunker down. The alarm had officially been sounded.

ARES Pittsburgh was under attack.

---

At the same moment that Cara and Tony emerged from the shooting range, Diana, Rath, and Max were curled up on the couch watching *Thor: Ragnarok* for the fourth or fifth time. The troll was in his tiny form, the better to mimic the movements on the screen. His chirpy voice echoed the best lines, and his delivery was flawless.

The Borzoi snored softly with his head resting lazily on his mistress' leg. Every so often, Diana would launch a sneak attack and hurl popcorn at the troll, and he would use his gymnastic skills to avoid them. She hadn't caught him yet but felt confident that he'd be distracted enough during the arena fight scene that a handful at once could nail him.

Her fingers sank deep into the bowl in preparation for that wicked intended assault a moment before the voices on the screen stretched into a slow, crawling pantomime.

*Danger.*

She couldn't sense where it came from. There was no directionality this time, and for an instant, she had no idea what to do. Instinct inspired her to reach out with her telekinesis and pull the tiny troll to her. The look of surprise on his face was momentarily amusing. She stood, turned in a circle, and enclosed them in a barrier.

The defense was barely completed before the front door was launched off its hinges and into the room at the same time as the large pair of windows that looked out onto the front yard exploded inward. On the far side of the dining area beside the living room, the sliding glass doors that led to the backyard transformed into a deadly hail of shards that careened toward them with deadly speed. The barrier she'd created held against those attacks, but she knew she wouldn't be able to sustain it against the witch and wizards who crossed the thresholds they'd created into her house.

She wasn't wearing a gun because she never did at home. The enemy's surprise assault had caught her totally unaware, and even with Rath's help, she couldn't defeat the five assailants who had come to kill them. She growled in anger and frustration, scooped the dog up, and bolted for the stairs. Thankfully, she was able to release the front portion of her shield and reinforce the one behind, and while the magic attacks pummeled it and drew her energy away, they didn't penetrate.

When they reached the bedroom, Diana set Max on his paws and flung the window open while Rath grew to his three-foot size and hauled the black escape rope from under her bed. It was secured to the frame's legs and was long enough to reach the ground, already knotted for ease of descent.

The forked lightning that seared through the open window was a near miss, but it still blistered the skin on the side of her neck and sent tingles through her body. "Shit. They planned well. Rath, any ideas?"

The troll shrugged, his expression grim. "Out the window and fight."

She nodded and stood again to release a blast of force at

the magic user on the ground. A wash of flame erupted from beside him, and she caught sight of several more casters outside. The fire alarms screeched and signaled the direness of the situation. She shook her head. "We can't stay in and can't go out. You know what that means."

Rath frowned. "Bad idea. Last resort."

"Thanks for the vote of confidence, little guy." She laughed and he grinned to show he was teasing. A section of the floor buckled and creaked beneath them as its support failed. "All right, let me concentrate."

She shut out the distractions one by one, grateful that the enemy had decided that burning them to death would be more entertaining than pursuing them up the stairs. She waved her hand in a circle, and a wavering image of Nylotte's shop appeared. The place looked downright cheerful compared to her flaming home. She focused on creating not only a window but a tunnel to protect them from interference. As the roof groaned alarmingly, she gathered Max and Rath in her arms and plunged into the portal scant seconds before the ceiling collapsed.

A flash of panic seized her as time seemed to skip and shudder. Had they failed? Would they fall into the World in Between? Would they be monster food?

The thoughts jostled wildly until the three of them collapsed on the floor of the Drow's shop. The woman herself stood over them, ready to attack or defend. Diana coughed out a weak, "Hi," and rolled onto her stomach to send a signal to the others. When she saw the Phalanx alert, she started the message relay she'd already set up with a young, scruffy Willen who lived on a nearby street, paying him with the small gold hoop earrings she was wearing. He would get the word out to the others.

"Status."

"I'm inbound to the base. However, Alfred tells me that everyone has checked in safely. Cara and Tony were the only ones attacked."

Diana breathed a sigh of relief. "Not the only ones, unfortunately. Call the fire department and send them to my house. Hopefully, they can keep it from spreading." She killed the connection, knowing that the systems built into the watch would show the tech where she was.

She chuckled and shook her head. *This is probably the safest place I could possibly be. No one wants to find themselves on Nylotte's bad side.*

Internal Diana countered immediately.

*Like she has a good side.*

As usual, Diana told her to shut up, then pushed herself off the ground to bring her teacher up to date and ask her for a portal out of the kemana.

*After all this nonsense, there's no way I'm walking up those damn stairs.*

# CHAPTER THIRTY-TWO

At first, the attacks had left Diana shaken. The realization that their personal lives were not off limits to their enemies was something she'd known intellectually but hadn't completely come to terms with. It was one of those thoughts that slid into her consciousness now and again but never really reached the front of the line for whatever reason. She spent a lot of time with Rath and Max in the extended-stay hotel, watching movies and generally trying to stay calm. The troll also seemed out of sorts, but honestly, who wouldn't be?

Nylotte had suggested she'd previously been in denial and had now had her eyes opened, but the observation had lacked her normal level of mockery and bordered on the sincere. That was perhaps the most frightening thing of all. Diana wasn't fond of the fact that she was walking around like an open wound but was grateful to her teacher, nonetheless.

After several days, shaken became angry. She marched

through the base, spent hours at the shooting range, and tried to stay away from others while she worked to master it. She got into a couple of serious battles with the Drow and relished the pain she felt after them. Internal Diana pointed out that this was probably because of the guilt she refused to release, but external Diana told her to shut her damn mouth and go to hell.

Another day passed, and she finally found her equilibrium again. She gave Rath a thirty-minute warning while she showered, dressed, and dried her hair. Then, they piled into the Fastback and drove for an hour and simply took roads at random, letting the vibe of the town soak into her bones again to replace the negative thoughts that had taken up residence in her brain. They swung past the house they'd rented, which was now nothing more than ashes and charred wood. Insurance would cover the building and their things, but that wasn't the point. She'd had roots, and the bastards had torn them out of the ground.

She decided in that moment to take the money she'd saved and put down deeper roots—buy a house and secure it so that no one could ever attack her that way again.

Rath loved the idea. "Oh, hell yes."

She looked at him with wide eyes. "Did you just swear at me?"

He grinned. "I've heard about another troll."

She groaned. "From who?"

"Kayleigh."

"I'll kill her."

He laughed and she pulled away from the curb and headed to the base. When she arrived, she and Rath walked directly to the second-floor lab. She barged in and folded her arms as she stared at the blonde technician. Kayleigh merely leaned back in her chair and returned the look with an expression of unlikely innocence on her face.

Diana's tone was accusatory. "You told him."

Kayleigh put a hand on her chest. "Moi? Told him what?"

"Don't play stupid."

She laughed. "I wondered how long it would be before you found out. Of course I told him. How could he not know about YTT?"

Diana sighed and sat on the worktable. "You'll destroy his innocence."

"Please. Words are nothing to be afraid of. Besides, I didn't tell him much at all. Including what those letters stand for."

She grinned at her. "You know that's not really why I'm here, right?"

Kayleigh nodded and sobered. "Yes."

"Listen, I understand if you don't want to, but—

The tech raised a hand to silence. "Yes. I'll stay. You need me, and I need the challenges you all present, given your many, many flaws. Besides, I take it personally when my friends are attacked."

Giddiness flowed over Diana, and she rushed forward to wrap the woman in a bear hug. After a moment of surprised resistance, she returned the gesture.

The agent stepped back. "I have some thoughts about combat tech."

She nodded. "I do, too. Good ones."

Rath beamed at them and clapped with smug satisfaction. "I will be Iron Troll."

*The story doesn't end here. Follow Diana, Rath and FAM's adventures in Agents of Chaos.*

## AGENTS OF CHAOS

The story doesn't end here. Follow Diana, Rath and FAM's adventures in Agents of Chaos

**AVAILABLE FOR PURCHASE HERE**

## CONNECT WITH TR CAMERON

Stay up to date on new releases and fan pricing by signing up for my newsletter. CLICK HERE TO JOIN.

Or visit: www.trcameron.com/Oriceran to sign up.

If you enjoyed this book, please consider leaving a review. Thanks!

# AUTHOR NOTES - TR CAMERON

## APRIL 28, 2019

Again and again, and over and over, thank you.

Thank you for reading the *third* book in the Federal Agents of Magic series, and for continuing on to the author notes! I've been blown away by the reviews and comments about the first couple books.

They helped me get through an April that was particularly challenging for me (I'm fully aware that what I find challenging, others might call a vacation. I'm lucky in a plethora of ways). The kiddo was sick. I was sick. Once I got done being sick, I lost the hearing in one of my ears for a week and a half, which sucked to an unexpected extent. Other life stuff was a bear. Finding the right frame of mind to work on this book was a challenge.

But it was also a lifeline. Visiting with these characters was the calm eye of my personal storm. Hopefully reading about them offers some of the same relaxation for you!

The upcoming books are going to be *big fun*. I can't wait to get them to you.

Spring is definitely in effect in my part of the world.

The dogwood tree in my front yard is throwing pretty white flowers all over the place. I see rabbits chasing each other through the overly-long grass, and feel the guilt-projecting looks of my neighbors standing in their perfectly trimmed lawns with their annoyed hands on their judgmental hips. *I have no idea why they dislike bunnies so much.* Weird neighborhood.

Our cats are obsessed with the wound-up birds outside the windows. None of them (there are five cats – long story – not my fault) does that cool chattering sound thing though. Too lazy, probably.

I'm very much looking forward to summer activities, to amusement parks and bike riding and trail walks, to time with family and friends. I hope your plans for the upcoming season wherever you live are excellent!

Today I'm getting the plot moments for Book 4 down on paper in their final form. Tomorrow I start writing. I'm as excited to start this one as I have been for any project, ever.

I'd like to give a loud and appreciative shout out to all the folks in the Oriceran editing team – the ones who catch my story holes or outright mistakes, the ones who make the words better, and the ones who notice when I've left in "ought" instead of "thought" despite my three rounds of editing. Not only does it make the final product better, but working with such a strong safety net lets me focus on story more, because I know the team's got my back.

Speaking of… ARES Pittsburgh is almost complete. We need a couple more pieces. The plan at this second is two more agents to finish up the team plus another tech, but we'll see how that works out. To quote Jayne Cobb from *Serenity* (to Mal): "Yeah, well what you plan and what takes place ain't ever exactly been similar." He's not wrong in my case, either.

Quick media notes: Avengers: Endgame *hurt*. The Battle of Winterfell *hurt*. As silly as it might sound, I think I'm actually doing some minor grieving for the characters I've loved and lost. (Parasocial interactions are a real thing, y'all). I'm catching up on CJ Cherryh's Foreigner series, which I got distracted from for a couple of years (Book 16 is on deck), and the next Brownstone book awaits on my Kindle app. I'm looking forward to *Watchmen* on HBO, *American Gods* (Mad Sweeny needs his own series), and *Good Omens*. Plus, *Deadwood*, but I fear what they're going to do to *that* set of beloved characters.

If you want to chat media, the books, or whatever else, I check in pretty often on Facebook. Just search TR Cameron Author to find me.

Until next time, Joys upon joys to you and yours – so may it be.

# AUTHOR NOTES - MARTHA CARR

## APRIL 29, 2019

The movies always make writing look like such a solitary undertaking and back when I had an agent and a publisher (and before the internet), it was. There was regular communication, but for the most part I was figuring out things by myself.

By the way, when it came to marketing, unless you were a big name and got a big advance, authors were still largely on their own to publicize their baby. They had the months leading up to publication and then three months after. If it didn't spark and create a sensation it left the bookshelves and that was it.

Authors occasionally saw each other at conferences – but those were mostly for book sellers, not the guys creating the books.

Then the internet came along, and all of us authors started talking more but it was still hit and miss. Mostly it was about what PR firm to use or avoid. We were still largely hands off, mostly doing things alone and we wouldn't have known how to help each other. I mean, how do I reach into another company and help your book?

But there was something brand new on the horizon. I still remember when Oprah had Jeff Bezos on her show with the first Kindle. It was revolutionary, but how much none of us really knew yet. (There's a good chance we're still in the creation phase of that and it'll be another generation that can look back and see the whole scope.)

Internet speeds picked up (remember dial up), and Amazon created Kindle Unlimited - a more affordable way to read as much as you wanted for just ten bucks a month - and a great way for some new author to get a chance to introduce themselves - to all of you.

That's what did it. Some pioneering writers decided to hack the system and write the books they wanted to write, put them out on their schedule (instead of the old spring and fall system), and keep the money. Covers were kind of well - bad at first and it took a while to catch on to the need for editing, and good blurbs, but the indie movement was up and rolling.

Then 20Books came along (a Facebook group for indie writers that focuses on marketing and is now 30k and growing). It was started by Michael Anderle and championed by Craig Martelle and it was like the last thing we really needed. A safe place to share ideas and ask questions. There's a strict no promo, no insults policy and just one infraction will get you tossed out.

Speaking as an author from pre-internet and watching the whole cycle of evolution - this was what was missing all along. A reservoir of knowledge that anyone can dip into - for free. Many of us owe our success to this group because we were able to ask questions, test things, come back when things failed – and sometimes collaborate even on the writing.

That's how we found TR Cameron – and what a find! A great writer who had some great stories in him to tell.

This all happened because a core group of authors were willing to share what they knew and were open to learning, changing, failing, trying again – and then sharing all of it all over again – for free. I've been there since about three hundred were in the group and I stayed to write with Michael because of something he was doing – not saying. He was just coming into his success and was offering to collaborate with pretty much anyone in those days. You have an idea? Are you willing to work for it? Are you open to listening to new ideas? Great, let's get going. I was one of those and every day I was surprised by his generosity and that he didn't suddenly draw a line and say, this is mine or how about me.

You have to be behind the scenes, deep bench, to see just how generous he is with his time and money. It's a credo that is carried by the rest of us as well and a characteristic we now look for in those we work with. Sure, we are and want to continue to be successful, but there's something more here. Still haven't reached the limits either and I hope I never do.

More adventures to follow.

## OTHER SERIES IN THE ORICERAN UNIVERSE:

SCHOOL OF NECESSARY MAGIC
SCHOOL OF NECESSARY MAGIC: RAINE CAMPBELL
ALISON BROWNSTONE
THE DANIEL CODEX SERIES
THE LEIRA CHRONICLES
I FEAR NO EVIL
FEDERAL AGENTS OF MAGIC
THE UNBELIEVABLE MR. BROWNSTONE
REWRITING JUSTICE
THE KACY CHRONICLES
MIDWEST MAGIC CHRONICLES
SOUL STONE MAGE
THE FAIRHAVEN CHRONICLES

OTHER BOOKS BY JUDITH BERENS

OTHER BOOKS BY MARTHA CARR

OTHER SERIES IN THE ORICERAN UNIVERSE:

## JOIN THE ORICERAN UNIVERSE FAN GROUP ON FACEBOOK!

## BOOKS BY MICHAEL ANDERLE

For a complete list of books by Michael Anderle, please visit

**www.lmbpn.com/ma-books/**

All LMBPN Audiobooks are Available at Audible.com and iTunes. For a complete list of audiobooks visit:

**www.lmbpn.com/audible**

www.ingramcontent.com/pod-product-compliance
Lightning Source LLC
Chambersburg PA
CBHW031648100726
47898CB00006B/2026